DOCTOR WHO AND THE
ANDROIDS OF TARA

DOCTOR WHO
AND THE
ANDROIDS OF TARA

Based on the BBC television serial by David Fisher by
arrangement with the British Broadcasting Corporation

TERRANCE DICKS

A TARGET BOOK
published by
the paperback division of
W. H. ALLEN & Co Ltd

A Target Book
Published in 1980
By the Paperback Division of W. H. Allen & Co. Ltd
A Howard & Wyndham Company
44 Hill Street, London W1X 8LB

Printed in Great Britain by
Richard Clay (The Chaucer Press), Ltd.,
Bungay, Suffolk

ISBN 0 426 201 086

Contents

The Doctor Goes Fishing

The Doctor was playing chess with K9.

In the control room of the TARDIS the centre column of the many-sided console rose and fell. Incredibly intricate machinery whirred, clicked and hummed speeding them through the space time continuum towards their next destination. That destination was now very close, though the Doctor was too absorbed to realise it. He leaned forward, made his move and started the chess clock.

K9 shook his head sadly. 'Inadvisable, Master.'

'What do you mean, inadvisable? I once saw Capablanca win the world championship with that move . . .'

'He lost.'

The Doctor stared indignantly down at the dog-like little automaton. '*Who* lost?'

'Capablanca.'

'You're sure?'

K9 was a mobile self-powered computer, and if there was one thing upon which he prided himself it was the accuracy of his data-banks. 'I have been programmed with all Earth Championship games since 1886. On the occasion to which you refer, Capablanca lost.'

The Doctor sighed. 'I must have missed the end of the game. It's your move, K9.'

'King to Knight's Two.'

'King to Knight's Two? That's a terrible move, weakens the King's side. Are you sure K9?'

'Affirmative.'

The Doctor made K9's move for him, and studied the board.

'Clock, Master,' reminded K9 reprovingly.

'I know, I know,' said the Doctor irritably, and started the clock. Suddenly things seemed to have become extraordinarily difficult, each possible move leading only to disaster. 'I think I'd better check your programming, K9, you're not supposed to be playing draughts,' he grumbled.

A tall, elegantly beautiful young woman came into the control room. Her name was Romana and she was a Time Lady, the Doctor's companion in recent adventures.

She looked disapprovingly at the scene before her. 'Doctor, what are you playing?'

'Playing chess, of course. Sssh, you'll spoil my concentration.'

'Aren't you forgetting something?'

The Doctor brooded over the chess-board. 'Very likely—only I can't seem to think what it is.'

'I am referring to our task, Doctor. The quest for the Key to Time—remember?'

For once in his long career the Doctor was embarked, not upon a series of random adventures, but on one continuous quest. He was searching for the six segments of the giant crystal that formed the Key to Time. In order to prevent it falling into the wrong hands, the Key had been split into six segments, scattered to distant parts of the universe.

But now the balance of the cosmos had been disturbed. A mysterious and powerful being called the White Guardian had given the Doctor the task of recovering the six segments and reassembling them into the Key to Time. Armed with this, the white Guardian would be able to restore the balance of the cosmos, and thwart the schemes of the evil Black Guardian to plunge the universe into chaos.

The Doctor was perfectly well aware of all this, but at the moment he wanted to forget it, at least for a while.

Romana, however, had a keenly developed sense of duty. She insisted on reminding the Doctor of the importance of their mission. 'The Guardian did stress the need for urgency, didn't he, Doctor?'

'Sssh! I'm trying to think.'

Romana moved across to the console. 'Shall I check the instrument readings, Doctor?'

'If you must ...' The Doctor looked up. 'I just feel we've earned a little break, that's all,' he said in an aggrieved voice. 'After all, we've got three of the six segments by now. I'd much rather play chess.'

'Really?' Romana studied the instrument readings. A wand-like device called the Tracer was plugged into the navigational circuits, steering the TARDIS to the part of the universe where the next segment could be found. The Tracer was a very necessary part of their search, since the divided segments had the power to disguise themselves as almost any imaginable, or unimaginable object.

'Almost there, Doctor,' said Romana briskly. 'We should be materialising in about ... fifteen seconds.'

'What about my game?'

Romana went over and looked at the board. 'Your game is already over, Doctor. Mate for K9 in twelve moves.'

'Correction, Mistress. Eleven moves.'

Romana looked again. 'Eleven? Yes, quite right. Sorry, K9.'

'Apologies not necessary, Mistress.'

'Mate in eleven?' Concentrating hard the Doctor ran all possible moves through his head, and then shook it in gloomy agreement. 'That's the trouble with chess, it's all so predictable.'

Romana's hands were moving over the controls. 'Materialisation commencing ... now. Five ... four ... three ... two ... The central column came to a halt, and Romana said proudly, 'Smooth enough for you, Doctor?'

The Doctor looked up in surprise. 'Arrived already, have we? A very creditable landing—for a beginner. Where are we?'

Romana gave him a withering look. 'On the planet Tara.' She began checking instrument readings with her usual efficiency. 'Earth-level gravity. Oxygen atmosphere. Temperate climate ...'

'Tara, eh?' said the Doctor thoughtfully. He flicked on the scanner and saw an attractive green landscape. Neatly-fenced fields, wooded hills—was that a castle on one of them? There was even a river, meandering peacefully across the countryside, its clear shallow waters sparkling in the sunshine.

The Doctor looked hard at the river. A thoughtful look came into his eyes. 'Tara, eh? Looks like a peaceful enough place. It shouldn't give you too much trouble.'

'Me? You mean us, don't you, Doctor?'

A rather guilty expression came over the Doctor's face. 'Aren't you going to get changed?'

Romana gave him a suspicious look, opened a door and went into one of the innumerable rooms adjoining the control room. Since the TARDIS was dimensionally transcendental—bigger on the inside than on the outside—the number of rooms it held was potentially infinite. So far Romana had seen only a fraction of them. She had acquainted herself with the wardrobe section though, and she made her way there now, sliding back a door to reveal a long cupboard, big enough to be a room in itself. Inside were racks holding coats and dresses and costumes of every imaginable period and planet. Romana walked through the racks, mentally checking off the codings. She stopped. 'Tara ... costume for Tara ... should be just about here.' She took a hanger from a rack and found it held a rustling grass skirt. She rechecked the coding on the hanger.

11

'Tara? No, Tahiti! Still, can't be far away!' She put the grass skirt back and went on searching.

The Doctor, meanwhile, was rooting through a cupboard in the main control room. It was a big corner cupboard, and it held an astonishing assortment of junk. He was always intending to store the stuff properly or get rid of it, but never seemed to get round to doing either. He heard Romana's voice behind him. 'What are you looking for?'

'I know it's here somewhere ...'

'What is?'

The Doctor pushed aside a medieval battle-axe and a partially-dismantled Martian sonic cannon, and found what he wanted. Seizing it triumphantly, he came out of the cupboard.

'Found it! Gosh this takes me back ... or is it forward? That's the trouble with time travel, you can never be sure.'

He was holding a long slender pole, with a kind of reel arrangement attached to the butt. The reel held fine thread, which was fed through loops attached to the pole.

Romana stared at the contraption in astonishment. 'What is it?'

'A fishing rod, of course. Last time I used this, I went out for the day with old Izaak Walton.'

The name of the great fishing writer meant nothing to Romana. She watched in astonishment, as the Doctor plunged back into the cupboard, emerging with a basket crammed with a clutter of mysterious-looking equipment. 'Everything's still here. Bit of a tangle, but I'll soon sort it out ...' He became aware that Romana was looking expectantly at him.

'Well, do you like it, Doctor?'

'Like what?'

'My new outfit.' Romana was wearing a flowing coat with wide lapels and a jaunty hat. The effect was rather like the riding costume of an Edwardian lady. 'According to our records it's what everyone's wearing on Tara this year, isn't it, K9?'

'Affirmative, Mistress.'

'Very nice,' said the Doctor absently, and returned his attention to the basket.

Fishing-rod over his shoulder, the Doctor strode out of the TARDIS and headed determinedly for the river.

Romana hurried after him. 'Where do you think you're going?'

'Fishing!'

'Another of those stupid sports you picked up on Earth?'

'Fishing is not stupid,' said the Doctor with dignity. 'And it's not a sport either, it's an art. An art, as dear old Izaak used to say, "worthy the knowledge and practice of a wise man".'

'We haven't got time for you to practice, Doctor. We've got to find the fourth segment of the Key to Time.'

'You find it,' said the Doctor cheerfully. 'I'm taking the day off.'

'You can't do that!' Romana was horrified at the Doctor's irresponsibility.

'Oh, can't I? Section ninety-three, paragraph two, Laws Governing the Conduct of Time Lords, says that a Time Lord, such as me, after a journey of more than four hundred years and twelve parsecs, is entitled to a period of rest and relaxation not exceeding fifty years.'

'*Does* it really say that?'

'Look it up!' The Doctor went on his way.

Romana hurried after him. 'I bet it doesn't at all. You're inventing it!'

They were still wrangling when they reached the banks of the river, a broad and shallow stream close to the edge of a shady wood.

The Doctor sat down with his back against a handy tree and began sorting through his fishing basket.

Romana looked down at him. 'You don't really want me to go on my own?'

'Why not? I don't see any sign of danger, do you? Lovely day, beautiful countryside. The walk will do you good.'

'Thank you very much!'

'Do you mind moving back a little? You're casting a shadow on the water. It frightens the fish.'

Romana tossed her head. 'Frightens the fish, indeed! Very well, Doctor, I *shall* go by myself. And I can tell you this—I shall *not* get myself involved in things that don't concern me, in the way that some people do!'

'Who me?'

Romana took the unplugged Tracer from under her coat and listened to its electronic note with an expert ear. She pointed to the wood. 'In my estimation the segment is in that direction, and not much more than a mile away. I shall go and get it, and return here in one hour. Be ready to leave.'

'Uh-huh,' said the Doctor absently. He began checking through an old tin box full of rusting fish-hooks.

Romana gave an indignant sniff and marched away.

The Tracer led her first along the river bank and then away from it into the wood. The path through the trees was winding and narrow, and it soon became narrower still. It began to rise steeply, and Romana realised she was climbing the side of a wooded hill.

Suddenly she began to feel uneasy. The trees seemed to crowd round her menacingly, and the canopy of leaves overhead reduced the sunlight to a dim green shade.

Suddenly, Romana became aware of a *sound*.

There was something moving in the undergrowth. Something that crashed through the bushes, snuffling and breathing heavily, always close by, yet always out of sight.

Romana began to run. The sounds kept pace.

The thing was tracking her.

She ran faster, and faster forcing her way through obstructing branches and bushes, her fear growing at each second then. To her immense relief, she burst out of the dark woods and into a sunlit clearing.

Gasping, she came to a halt, and looked around her. In the centre of the clearing were the traces of some ruined building. Perhaps an ancient temple had stood there long ago. Now all that remained were the foundations, a few tumbled blocks of stone ... and the statue.

It stood on a battered plinth, a vaguely dragon-like heraldic beast, thrusting time-blunted claws towards the blue summer sky. Statue and plinth alike were eroded by weather and time.

Romana held out the Tracer and the electronic note rose to maximum pitch. The fourth segment to the Key to Time was *here*. Hidden in the statue, perhaps? Or, since the segments had the power of transmutation, perhaps it *was* the statue.

Romana reached out and touched the plinth of the statue. Nothing happened.

She touched the statue itself. There was a blurring and shimmering and suddenly the statue was gone. In its place was a large, irregularly shaped chunk of crystal—the fourth segment of the Key to Time.

Romana gave a smile of satisfaction, and picked it up. This would show the Doctor how efficient she was. A short walk through the woods, and she could drag the Doctor away from his silly fishing. Then, back to the TARDIS and on with the quest for the fifth segment. None of those ridiculous irrelevant adventures *he* always got mixed up in ...

In her excitement, Romana had forgotten the rustling sounds she had heard earlier.

The sounds returned, louder now, as some great beast thrust its way through the forest.

There was a savage roar, and Romana whirled round.

A wild animal rushed towards her out of the woods.

2

Count Grendel

The monster was a good eight feet tall—and it walked upright like a man. It had coarse black fur, slavering jaws filled with yellow, pointed teeth and a stubby horn projecting from the centre of its forehead. A mixture of bear, ape and boar, with the nastiest features of all three.

Not that Romana was familiar with these Earth animals. She wasn't familiar with animals of any kind. Before joining up with the Doctor she had spent her life in the vast Time Lord city-complex called the Capitol.

Romana backed away, until she was pressed against the plinth. She tried to call upon her Time Lady training in detachment; when confronted with the reality of a slavering monster, it wasn't so easy.

The creature paused. Presumably it had never seen anything like Romana before, and it was wondering if she was dangerous.

Romana considered making a dash for the woods. No, the monster would be able to cut her off before she got to the edge of the clearing. Even if she did reach the forest, it would overhaul her and pull her down ...

Romana sidled round the plinth, trying to get the stone pillar between them. But the creature sensed her plan and moved sideways with her.

It threw back its head and gave a roar of challenge, preparing to charge ...

Another, larger, monster appeared from the forest. Or so it seemed at first. Then she realised it was a man on horseback. The horse was richly decorated with ornamental trappings, a gorgeous saddle-cloth and a huge elaborate saddle. The rider was even more impressive. He wore a military-style uniform not unlike that of a nineteenth-century hussar, and a plumed helmet.

The rider halted his horse at the edge of the clearing and dismounted.

The creature swung round to face this new threat, roaring out its challenge.

The horseman drew his sword and advanced to meet it. The sword was a long, slender rapier, and it looked terribly light-weight in the face of this ravening monster. Something like a battleaxe would be more appropriate, decided Romana, or better still a good heavy-duty blaster.

The monster charged, the swordsman lunged, and Romana saw that this was no ordinary weapon. As it touched the monster, there was a sizzling crackle and a shower of sparks. The creature leaped back with a roar of pain.

Recovering its courage, it attacked again. The swordsman sidestepped a blow from its great slashing paw, and thrust again ... There was another shower of sparks and again the monster retreated.

It was a kind of electro-sword, Romana realised, and the slender metal blade carried a powerful energy-charge ...

But it didn't seem strong enough to kill the monster, or even stun it. It only seemed to be making it angrier.

As she watched the combat, Romana realised the swordsman didn't want to kill the beast. He was playing with it amusing himself, using his skill to dodge the murderous claws, retaliating with jab after jab from his sword. Before long, the monster had had enough. With a last roar of anger and frustration, it turned and lumbered away into the forest.

Sword in hand Romana's rescuer walked towards her. He was tall, broad shouldered and heavily moustached. His darkly handsome face was marred only slightly by a fiercely jutting beak of a nose. He seemed utterly astonished at the sight of Romana. He stood there, staring into her face as if he couldn't believe his eyes. 'Incredible ...'

Romana decided to put things on a proper social footing. 'I really don't know how to thank you. That creature would have killed me if you hadn't arrived. May I know your name?'

The man laughed. '*My* name? That's rich! Are you damaged?'

'No, I don't think so. Just a bit shaken.'

'You're sure your *head* isn't injured?' He was still staring into her face.

Romana rubbed the back of her head. 'No, I don't think so. There's no harm done, really. Won't you tell me who you are?'

The man looked at her, a quizzical half smile on his lips, but he didn't reply.

'Look, I'm sorry if you're someone frightfully important, but I'm a stranger round here. My name is Romana.'

The man sheathed his sword and bowed. 'The fair Romana. That's a pretty name.' His voice was deep, and a little hoarse.

'Thank you. Tell me, are there many wild animals like that around here? I understood Tara was relatively civilised.'

'It is, I assure you. I keep a few of the beasts in my woods—for the hunting, you know. They don't usually attack anyone, not unless they're frightened in some way.'

'*Your* woods?'

The man gestured expansively. 'All this is part of the estate of Gracht—or rather, what was left, after my father's debts were paid ... What happened to the statue?'

Romana looked at the empty plinth. The crystal segment of the Key to Time was still resting on its centre. 'I've no idea. Is it important?'

The man frowned. 'Only to superstitious peasants. It is my family emblem, reputed to guard our fortunes, or at least, it was. How very odd.' Before Romana could stop him, he reached out and picked up the crystal, weighing it in his hand. 'A curiously shaped stone.'

'Yes, isn't it?' Determined to recover the crystal, Romana took a step towards him—then stopped, wincing as pain shot through her ankle.

The man reached out to steady her, taking hold of her arm. His grip was very strong. 'You've damaged your ankle.'

'It's nothing, really. Could I have my stone?'

'*Your* stone?'

'I found it ... nearby. I collect crystal, it's a kind of hobby. Could I have it back, please?'

'Of course ... as soon as it's been registered.'

'Registered?'

'Yes, of course. Do you not know the law? It is decreed that all minerals, particularly unusual ones like this, must be registered with the Knight of Castle Gracht.'

'And who is that?'

'Me! I am Count Grendel, Knight of Gracht, Master of the Sword.'

'I see. Will it take long?'

'The merest formality,' Count Grendel assured her smoothly. 'More important, is the fact that your ankle needs attention.'

'Really, it's nothing.' Romana hobbled a few steps and winced.

Count Grendel waved her protestations aside. 'I shall take you to my castle. My steward can register the stone while my surgeon attends to your injury.

Then I'll provide you with a mount, and an escort to wherever you like.'

'You're very kind, but it's a question of time——'

'An hour, no more,' said the Count masterfully. 'What's an hour out of your life?' Before Romana could protest further, he said firmly. 'I shall not take no for an answer.' He stepped forward and picked her up in his arms, carrying her towards his horse, which stood patiently waiting at the edge of the clearing.

Romana looked at the great beast in some alarm. She wasn't used to domesticated animals either. 'What's that?'

'My favourite charger. Strong as a tree, swift as the wind! Come!'

He swung Romana up on to the saddle-bow and mounted behind her. Steadying her with an arm around her waist, he took the reins with the other hand, touched spurs to the horse's flanks.

The great horse began to move and Romana said nervously, 'What a splendid creature.' She wondered if the animal really was just an animal. Technology on Tara seemed a strange mixture of the primitive and advanced. The sword hadn't really been just a sword. Perhaps the horse was more than a horse, some kind of robot. 'How does it work?' she asked cautiously. 'I mean, what makes it go?'

Count Grendel laughed. 'Good heavens, I don't know, my dear.'

'You don't?'

'I'm a knight, not a farrier! Hold tight!' They had

reached a broad path leading away from the clearing. The Count put spurs to his horse, and they thundered away.

It was all rather ridiculous really, thought Romana. Like one of those romantic videonovels she'd viewed when she was very young. Still, it was an amusing little incident, and it would soon be over. As the Count's charger carried her away, Romana made a mental apology to the Doctor. Local complications were not as easy to avoid as she had believed.

The Doctor woke up and found that his hat was on fire. He'd been sleeping peacefully a few minutes earlier, his fishing rod propped up by a cleft stick, the float bobbing lazily in the stream. The Doctor dozed, his hand resting on the butt of the rod, confident the vibration of a catch would wake him up—if he got a bite. There'd been no sign of one so far. Maybe the fish of Tara didn't like old Izaak's bait ...

What woke him was not the quivering of the rod but the smell of burning cloth. He opened his eyes, and saw the blade of a slender metal sword brushing across the brim of his hat, leaving a trail of sparks behind it. The Doctor snatched off his hat and beat it on the ground. A booted foot was thrust against his chest, and the sword-tip hovered inches from his nose.

The Doctor looked up. Two men were standing over him, one young, one middle-aged, both elaborately uniformed in the style of Earth's nineteenth century.

The younger man, the one with the drawn sword, wore an elaborate metal helmet.

'I say, would you mind not standing on my chest?' said the Doctor politely.

The two men stared impassively down at him.

'I don't think we've met before.'

Still no one spoke.

The Doctor tried again. 'Look, is it something I've said? Or done?' He snapped his fingers. 'I know—I'm poaching! I'm sorry I didn't ask permission, but I didn't see any "No Fishing" notices.'

The older man spoke. 'Who are you?' He had the harsh, stern voice of a man accustomed to command.

'They usually call me the Doctor . . .'

'What are you doing here?'

'Oh, just a flying visit!' The Doctor rolled away from the younger man's boot. Before anyone realised what was happening, he was on his feet. 'I'm just passing through.'

'This is Prince Reynart's hunting estate.'

'It is? Well, I didn't know, did I? I told you, I didn't see any "No Fishing" notices. Anyway, I didn't catch anything, if that's any help. See for yourself, nothing in the basket, nothing on the hook.' The Doctor reeled in his line. 'Not even bait,' he added ruefully.

The helmeted young man raised his sword. 'Shall I kill him, Swordmaster Zadek?'

'Not until *I* give the order, Swordsman Farrah.'

'That really won't be necessary,' said the Doctor hurriedly. 'If there's a fine, I'll be more than happy to pay it.' He began groping in his pocket, but realised he didn't have any local currency—or any other kind of currency for that matter. He picked up his hat and examined the charred brim. 'How did that happen? Incendiary moths?'

Farrah was still holding his sword at the Doctor's chest. The Doctor reached out and touched the sword-tip with one finger, snatching it away as he felt the tingle of power.

'May I?' he said politely, and his long arm flashed out. Before the outraged young man realised what was happening the sword had been twisted neatly from his hands.

The Doctor examined the weapon thoughtfully. 'I see. Electrically charged blade. Power pack in the hilt, I suppose?' He tossed the weapon back. The astonished Farrah caught it, and promptly pointed the sword at the Doctor's chest.

'You know about machines? Electronics?' Zadek pronounced the words distastefully, as if the subject was really rather beneath him.

'I know a bit about most things,' said the Doctor modestly.

'Strange. You do not look like a peasant.'

'Well, of course I don't. Me? A peasant?'

Zadek looked thoughtfully at him. 'Nevertheless, you do have certain skills? Can you mend an android?'

'What's wrong with it?'

'It won't go,' said Zadek simply.

'Look, I'd love to help you, I really would. But I'm

a bit pressed for time at the moment. Why don't you just get in touch with your local android dealer?'

The Doctor broke off. Farrah had lunged smoothly forward, and the tip of the electro-sword was less than an inch from his throat. '*Now* shall I kill him?'

'On second thoughts,' said the Doctor brightly, 'why don't we go and take a look at that android?'

3

The Double

The forest track, rose, broadened and turned into a narrow winding road, which led them to the gates of a castle on a hill. It was a gloomy, forbidding place, surrounded by a moat. Its towers and battlements rose blackly against the skyline, and seemed to cast a shadow over the peaceful green countryside below.

'Castle Gracht, my dear,' said Count Grendel proudly. 'Ancient home of the Grendels of Gracht.'

'It's beautiful,' said Romana politely.

'Yes, it is, isn't it. And quite, quite escape-proof, I'm happy to say!' With that, Count Grendel set spurs to his horse and galloped over the drawbridge. The portcullis rose automatically as they rode towards it. The Count rode into the cobbled courtyard beyond and reined to a halt.

Romana heard a low rumbling sound behind her. Glancing over her shoulder, she saw the portcullis-gate coming down again, huge bolts sliding into place to secure it. The defences of Castle Gracht were automatic, electronically operated, a strange mixture of ancient tradition and modern technology that was typical of Tara.

A grotesque figure ran out of an arched stone door-way and scuttled towards them, taking the reins of the charger. It was a dwarf, immensely broad and strong, wearing rough leather garments. 'My servant Till,' said Grendel briefly. He swung down from his horse and lifted Romana down after him, still holding her in his arms. 'There, that wasn't too bad was it?'

'There's no need to carry me, you know. I can still walk!'

Count Grendel ignored her. 'Till, see to my horse. And summon Madame Lamia!'

Till bowed and tugged at his forelock. 'Yes, Master.' He led the horse away.

Count Grendel carried Romana through the arched doorway, along a maze of gloomy stone corridors. 'Madame Lamia is my surgeon. She'll take care of you.'

He carried her into a stone walled chamber. There were bars on the windows and flagstones on the floor, but the room was brightly lit and its walls were lined with complex technological equipment. It felt like a cross between an operating theatre and a dentist's surgery, and Romana didn't like the look of it at all.

Count Grendel laid her down on a low couch. 'There you are! Madame Lamia will be here in a moment.'

'Thank you. You won't forget to register my stone, will you?'

'Stone? Oh yes, the crystal.' Count Grendel tapped his belt-pouch. 'I'll see to it in a moment. Ah, there you are, Lamia!'

A tall, dark-haired woman came into the room. She wore a severe white robe and she was strikingly attractive in an intense almost angry way. 'I received your message, my lord.' Her tone was respectful, but only just.

The Count smiled at Romana. 'This is Madame Lamia, my surgeon-engineer.'

Lamia was staring at Romana in utter astonishment. 'That face—I don't believe it!'

'What's the matter with it?' asked Romana indignantly.

Lamia looked at the Count. 'It's incredible, a marvellous job. Who made it?'

'The question is not so much *who*, as *why*?'

Lamia shrugged. 'I'm a peasant, I leave politics to my betters.'

Count Grendel touched her cheek. 'Very wise of you, my dear.'

Madame Lamia's eyes flashed angrily, but she said nothing, standing quite still under Count Grendel's touch.

Romana looked curiously at them both, puzzled by the tension between them. It was obvious that they were more to each other than master and servant—and something else was obvious too. For all her fiercely independent spirit, Madame Lamia was frightened of the Count. Romana decided she'd had enough of this strange pair. She sat up. 'Look, I've no idea what you two are talking about, and I think it's time I left.'

'Restrain her, Lamia,' said Count Grendel coldly.

Madame Lamia took Romana by the shoulders and thrust her back on the couch. Romana struggled wildly, but the dark woman was astonishingly strong. Count Grendel touched a control and broad iron clamps arched up over Romana's body, clamping her to the couch.

'What do you want me to do with her, my lord?'

Count Grendel leaned over Romana, and took her head between his hands, studying it thoughtfully.

'We can't have her running about the kingdom, can we? You'd better disassemble her. Perhaps we can cannibalise her for parts. I should like to keep her head, though. You're right, it really is a marvellous job.'

Romana stared wildly at them, wondering if she'd fallen into the hands of a pair of murderous lunatics.

To her horror she saw Lamia take a piece of equipment from a rack on the wall. It was a long, fine-toothed electrical hand-saw. It whirred menacingly as Lamia switched it on.

Madame Lamia put down the saw, picked up a soft-tipped marking pen, and used it to draw a neat circle around Romana's neck. 'I shall make the incision *here*, I think.'

Count Grendel smiled. 'Excellent! I always enjoy watching you work, my dear.'

'Thank you, my lord.' Madame Lamia picked up the electro-saw again and leaned over Romana.

Romana summoned up all the icy dignity of a Time Lady. 'Far be it from me to question this lady's competence, Count Grendel, but where I come from you don't cure a sprained ankle by cutting off the patient's head!'

Lamia paused, the whirring saw inches from Romana's throat. 'Ankle?'

'There was some kind of minor damage to its ankle,' said Count Grendel casually.

Lamia switched off the saw, moved to the edge of the couch and ran her fingers over Romana's ankles. In an incredulous voice she said. 'Her left ankle appears to be swollen!'

'Well, of course it is,' said Romana. 'What did you expect?'

Lamia turned to the Count. 'My lord, she is not an android.'

'What?'

'Android plasti-flesh does not bruise or swell. This girl is real!'

'Oh, brilliant,' muttered Romana.

Count Grendel leaned over Romana and stroked her cheek. 'In that case, you may keep your pretty head on your body, my dear. I have a use for both!'

The Doctor was taken to a secluded hunting lodge in the forest, a simple two-storey structure built from carved wooden logs.

Zadek climbed the short flight of steps that led to the front door and went inside, the Doctor followed and the young man, Farrah, came after them, his sword point levelled at the Doctor's back.

The Doctor found himself in a big wood-panelled room which took up most of the lower floor of the house. A long table ran down its centre of the room, surrounded by heavy wooden chairs with high ornately carved backs. There was an assortment of comfortable chairs arranged around a stone fireplace, and at the rear of the room a short flight of steps gave access to a balcony and a number of doors, presumably leading to the sleeping quarters. Zadek went up the steps, and disappeared through the central door.

As the Doctor stood looking around him, a shove between the shoulder-blades sent him staggering into the centre of the room. He turned round angrily and saw Farrah grinning at him from the doorway.

The Doctor tried to move forward, and found he couldn't. 'Do you mind,' he said mildly. 'You're treading on my scarf!'

Farrah's sword flashed in an arc of light, and the charred end of the Doctor's scarf dropped smoking to the floor.

The Doctor took a step towards Farrah. 'If you go on doing that, you're going to *have* to kill me!'

There was a sword in Farrah's hand and the Doctor was unarmed—but suddenly Farrah was frightened.

A voice from the balcony said, 'Do forgive Swordsman Farrah. He tends towards over-enthusiasm, particularly in the service of his Prince.'

The Doctor turned. Zadek had returned to the balcony. With him was a slender, handsome man in an

33

elaborate gold-trimmed uniform.

The Doctor scowled at the singed end of his scarf. 'Well, he'd better be good at knitting, that's all!'

'Speak with respect, peasant,' snapped Zadek. 'You address Prince Reynart of Tara.'

The Doctor made an elaborate bow. 'Honoured, Your Highness.' He glared at Zadek. 'I keep telling you, I am not a peasant.'

The Prince came down the steps. 'But you do know how to repair an android?'

'That depends.'

Zadek's hand went to the hilt of his sword. 'Upon what?'

The Prince put a restraining hand on Zadek's arm. 'Upon how well we treat him! Of course you are no peasant, Doctor. Very well, let me make you an offer. Five hundred gold pieces if you will mend our android.'

'If you think I can be bought——' began the Doctor angrily, then stopped himself. If he refused their money, these fools would simply offer him more. If that didn't work, they would try to force him to help them by threats. Simpler to take the money, do the job and go. 'You did say five hundred gold pieces?'

'I did.'

'Done! But suppose I can't manage to repair your android?'

'Then we shall let Swordsman Farrah have you for sword practice!' snarled Zadek.

Prince Reynart laughed. 'We shall do no such thing,

Zadek. This man is obviously a gentleman. If he can mend our android we shall reward him. If he cannot ...' He smiled pleasantly at the Doctor. 'I give you my word, whatever happens you will not be harmed. You can go free.'

'Thank you very much,' said the Doctor and headed for the door.

Farrah sprang to bar his way.

'Not yet, Doctor,' said Prince Reynart smoothly. 'First the android.'

'All right, let's see it!'

The Prince nodded to Zadek, who swept back a curtain to reveal a wheeled trolley. Upon it lay a motionless, blank-faced figure. 'There he is, Doctor.'

The Doctor removed the inspection plate from the android's head and began checking the separate circuits, one by one. 'Not a bad piece of work—mind you, I've seen better.'

The Prince watched in fascination. 'Don't you sometimes wish, Zadek, that custom permitted *us* to learn these skills?'

'With respect, no, Your Highness. Had we been meant to learn peasant skills, we'd have been born peasants.'

Prince Reynart sighed, a little regretfully. 'Perhaps you're right.'

It was an interesting exchange, the Doctor thought, and one which revealed much about Taran society. Technological skills had been developed, but had remained in the hands of the peasant classes. The aristocracy had clung to its traditions, ruling in the same old-fashioned ways. Perhaps it wasn't so very strange after all. A medieval knight had to know how to use a sword, but no one expected him to be able to *make* one. Even in Queen Victoria's navy, Engineering Officers had been regarded as a lower form of life.

Prince Reynart's voice broke in on his reflections. 'Well, Doctor? Can our android be repaired?'

'That depends what you want him to do.'

Zadek came forward with a plastic case, which he passed to the Prince.

Prince Reynart opened the case and held it out to the Doctor. 'For one thing, he must wear this!'

A face looked at the Doctor out of the box, or rather a face-mask. It bore the features of Prince Reynart.

The Doctor looked from the mask to Prince Reynart's face. 'Why? Why do you need an android double?'

'Tomorrow, I am to be crowned King of Tara. The ceremony will take place at the appropriate hour, fixed by the Court Astrologers, in the great Coronation Room in the Palace of Tara.'

The Doctor bowed. 'Congratulations, Your Majesty.'

Prince Reynart smiled wryly. 'The congratulations, and the title will be in order only if I reach the Coronation Room alive.'

'Who's going to stop you?'

'Count Grendel of Gracht, if he can. He'll kill me if necessary. You can't crown a dead prince. But the first thing he'll do is to post men watching every entrance to the Palace, to prevent me from arriving on time. And if they succeed in delaying me ...'

'Would it be so serious? I thought Kings were allowed to be late?'

'Not on Tara. If I fail to appear at precisely the right moment it will be taken that the stars do not favour my accession. I shall lose my right to the crown.'

'And I take it Count Grendel of Gracht is the next in line?'

'The only other contender for the throne is the Princess Strella—she disappeared some time ago.'

The Doctor indicated to the android. 'And where does George here fit into all this?'

It was Zadek who replied. 'There have already been three attempts on His Highness's life. The next one could be successful.'

'So you plan to let them attack George instead?'

Prince Reynart nodded eagerly. 'Precisely. We use George—that is to say, we use my android copy—to create a diversion, distract their attention.'

'Draw their fire?' suggested the Doctor helpfully.

Zadek said grimly. 'We've already tried the scheme once—the android took the Prince's place in a hunting party. There was an assassin in the forest with a crossbow. The Prince escaped unhurt, but the android fell when its horse bolted.'

'We feared it was damaged beyond repair,' explained Prince Reynart. 'Now, thanks to you Doctor, we can use the android to draw Grendel's fire while I slip past his guards into the Coronation Room. Do you think the plan will work, Doctor?'

'A substitute Prince, eh?' The Doctor smiled. 'Why not—it's been done before!'

'I don't like it,' protested Madame Lamia.

Count Grendel smiled. 'I don't ask you to like it. Just do it!'

'But think of the risk, my lord. Is it wise?'

'Do you question my commands?'

'No, my lord, of course not. Have I not proved my loyalty a thousand times?'

'Then do as I tell you, or I shall have you flogged,' said Count Grendel with a kind of silky brutality. 'And don't imagine that I won't.'

Madame Lamia went pale. 'Very well, my lord.' She crossed to a wall cabinet and took out a syringe.

Clamped to the table, Romana looked on in horror, as Madame Lamia filled the syringe from a phial of colourless fluid and came towards her.

'No!' she gasped. 'What do you think you're doing?' She felt Lamia rolling back her sleeve, there was the prick of an injection, and a few seconds later, Romana floated away on a cloud of darkness.

The immaculately uniformed figure at the table raised its glass in salute. 'Congratulations, Doctor, and thank you. Now I must retire. Goodnight, gentlemen.' The figure put down its glass, rose and went up to the balcony and disappeared through one of the doors.

Prince Reynart watched his android replica depart. 'Excellent. Farrah, bring more wine.'

Farrah hastened to obey.

The Prince turned to the others. 'You know, it's eerie seeing yourself walk and talk. I never thought you'd be able to get it going again, Doctor.'

'It'll do all right for a time, Your Majesty, but it's only patched up. If I had the proper tools . . .'

'Never mind, it's good enough to fool Grendel's men, eh, Zadek?'

'I sincerely hope so, Your Highness—for all our sakes.'

'Always the pessimist, Zadek! We owe you our thanks, Doctor. Zadek?'

Zadek put a leather pouch on the table. 'Five hundred gold pieces.'

As the Doctor slipped the money into his pocket, Prince Reynart said, 'You wouldn't be interested in a permanent post, Doctor, once I am King?'

The Doctor shook his head firmly. 'Sorry, but I'm otherwise engaged.' It was about time he found out what had happened to Romana.

Farrah came up from the cellar with a tray which held glasses and a dusty wine bottle.

'A pity, Doctor,' said Prince Reynart smoothly. 'Still, at least you'll join us in a toast to our success?'

'Well, I don't usually indulge,' said the Doctor. 'Perhaps just a small one.'

Farrah poured the wine and handed round the glasses.

'Just one of our local wines, Doctor,' said the Prince,

'But I think you'll find it palatable.'

Zadek raised his glass. 'With your permission, Your Highness—to the King!'

The others raised their glasses. 'The King!'

The Doctor didn't think much of the local wine— it had a curiously bitter tang to it—but he drained his glass politely and set it down.

Farrah tried to do the same. Somehow he missed the table and his glass fell to the floor. Seconds later, Farrah fell as well.

'Must be pretty potent stuff,' said the Doctor owlishly. He was feeling a little strange himself.

Prince Reynart gasped, clutched at his throat and collapsed.

'Treachery!' growled Zadek. He reached for his sword, but he was unconscious before the weapon left the sheath.

The Doctor felt as if his legs had turned to lead. He rose and staggered towards the door, each step costing him enormous effort.

The door seemed to recede before him. To his astonishment he saw that it was opening.

The Doctor crashed to the ground, falling at the feet of the man who had just entered the room.

Count Grendel of Gracht stepped over the Doctor's body and came into the room, his men at his heels.

He looked down at the unconscious body of Prince Reynart and smiled.

4

The Princess

A savage jab from a booted foot jerked the Doctor from his drugged sleep. He looked up to see a uniformed figure looming over him. The Doctor groaned, and shook his aching head. 'So much for the local brew.'

His vision cleared and he saw without much surprise that it was Farrah who was kicking him. 'Wake up, traitor! I want you to be quite conscious when I kill you!'

The Doctor struggled slowly to his feet. Farrah drew his sword. 'Oh, go away,' said the Doctor wearily. 'Haven't you got anything better to do?'

'Only one thing's stopping me from running you through right now!'

'And what's that?'

'I want to know where he is.'

The Doctor collapsed into a chair. 'Where who is? What the devil are you talking about?'

Farrah raised his sword.

A voice snapped. 'That's enough, Farrah!' Zadek came down the steps from the rear balcony. His tunic collar was unbuttoned and his hair dishevelled; it was obvious that he'd been splashing water on his face.

'The Prince has gone, Doctor. Vanished. He's been kidnapped.'

'Who by? Sorry, I mean, by whom?'

It was Farrah who answered. 'By your master, Count Grendel. Who else?'

'Look, I realise this is going to come as an awful shock to you, but I don't even know the Count.'

'I'm inclined to believe you, Doctor,' said Zadek.

'Thank you.'

'But Swordmaster——' protested Farrah.

'Oh, use your intelligence, Farrah. If the Doctor was involved, why would he remain behind once the Prince had been taken? It doesn't make sense.'

The Doctor got up and went into the bedroom. A moment later he was back, carrying the android. He dumped it in a chair. 'At least they didn't take George.'

'They took the real Prince,' said Zadek bitterly. 'What use is the copy now?'

The Doctor looked thoughtfully at him. 'It depends what you're going to do.'

'We shall do what honour demands.'

'What's that?'

'Swordsman Farrah and I will take our swords and do battle with the Count's men.'

'Just the two of you?'

'Us and a handful of others. The Prince has first claim to the throne, but his house is old and impoverished. We cannot hire mercenaries like Grendel. Besides, Castle Gracht is almost impregnable ...'

'So you'll probably all get killed?'

Farrah drew himself up. 'A Swordsman does not fear death, if he dies with honour.'

'Then he's an idiot,' said the Doctor cheerfully. 'Let me see if I understand the situation. In order to be crowned King, the Prince *must* present himself at the Coronation Room at precisely the appointed hour, right?'

Zadek nodded stiffly. 'That is correct.'

'Then there's no problem.' The Doctor nodded towards the android. 'You've still got a Prince. Get him to the Coronation Room and have *him* crowned.'

Zadek was horrified. 'Crown an android King of Tara? Never?'

'Would you rather crown Count Grendel?'

Farrah too was shocked. 'But an android—it's unthinkable.'

Zadek was over his shock and was beginning to consider the plan seriously. 'Even if we tried, Doctor, Grendel's men would still try to stop us getting into the Coronation Room.'

The Doctor sensed Zadek was holding something back. 'You'd have faced that problem anyway, if you're outnumbered, I don't imagine Prince Reynart was planning to walk in through the front door, was he?'

'The Prince had a plan.'

'Well?'

Almost reluctantly, Zadek said, 'There is a hidden passage ...'

'Does Grendel know about it?'

'I hope not. It is an old secret of the Prince's family.'

The Doctor grinned. 'You know, I thought it might be something like that. Well, there you are, then. I'll do a bit more work on the android, and you and Farrah can take him along and get him crowned. Grendel will be thrown into confusion, and the android can rule the country long enough for you to find the real Prince. It's worth a try, isn't it?'

Zadek frowned. 'I can see two obstacles to your plan, Doctor.'

'Only two? What are they?'

'What if the android breaks down again?'

'Well, it's possible, I admit. What's the second problem?'

'Security. If the slightest hint of our scheme gets out, it will mean disaster.'

'I don't see that that's a problem. Only the three of us here need ever know anything about it.'

'Precisely. Farrah, I know I can trust. But you, Doctor——'

'Don't worry. I'll be light years away by the time George is King of Tara.'

Zadek smiled grimly. 'No, Doctor. You see, I have thought of a way to deal with *both* problems. You will remain with the android at all times.'

'Oh no, Zadek. I've got more important things to do than get mixed up in the politics of your piffling little planet.'

Farrah's sword flashed out and the point hovered inches from the Doctor's throat. 'On the other hand,' said the Doctor thoughtfully, 'I could just stay with the android at all times.'

Romana was quite right, he thought ruefully. He really must stop getting mixed up in other people's problems.

Farrah watched suspiciously, as the Doctor went over to the door, opened it, took a small metal object from his pockets, put it to his lips and blew. The surprising thing was that there was no sound.

'What are you doing?'

'I'm calling my dog.'

'I don't see any dog,' said Farrah puzzled.

'Don't worry. You will!'

Inside the TARDIS, K9 came suddenly to life. His head lifted, his tail antenna wagged and his eye-screens lit up. 'Master?' K9 moved his head to and fro, fixing the direction from which the subsonic signal was coming. Then he sent out a signal of his own, one which operated the remote-control setting of the TARDIS doors. The doors swung open, and K9 glided away.

The Doctor was rechecking his work on the android, wondering if it would stand up to the strains ahead. After all, when he'd repaired it, no one had told him it was to be crowned King of Tara.

Zadek was watching anxiously. 'Everything is in order?'

'Well, apart from the fact that half his microcircuitry's burnt out, his bio-mechanisms's on the blink and his powerpacks seem to need constant recharging —yes!'

'I have every confidence in your work——' began Zadek.

'I'm deeply touched!'

'But remember, either Farrah or myself will be with you at all times. Don't let us down—will you, Doctor?'

The Doctor sighed. He was getting rather fed up with being threatened. 'Now look here, Zadek——'

A familiar voice interrupted him. 'You called, Master?' K9 was standing in the doorway.

Zadek swung round in alarm. 'What is that thing?'

'Thing?' repeated the Doctor indignantly. 'That's my dog!'

'But it's a machine!'

'Well? So's your Prince, isn't he?'

With his usual reaction to any new threat, Farrah drew his sword and advanced on K9.

'I really wouldn't do that, old chap,' advised the Doctor. 'K9 doesn't like being threatened either, do you, K9?'

Ignoring the warning, Farrah waved his blade threateningly. K9 raised his head, gave an electronic growl, and fired a low-intensity blast from his photon-blaster.

Farrah gave a yell, and dropped the sword as if it had suddenly become red-hot.

The Doctor grinned. 'I hate to say I told you so— but I told you so!' He bent down and patted K9. 'Where's Romana? I thought she'd come with you.'

'The Mistress has not yet returned, Master.'

'What? She was only supposed to be an hour—and that was yesterday!'

'You have lost a companion, Doctor?' asked Zadek.

'My assistant, Romana. She went off to look for something.'

'What?'

'Never you mind.'

'Tara can be a dangerous place for strangers. Where did you see her last?'

'Close to where you two picked me up.'

'Which way did she go?'

'I'm not sure. Away up the hill somewhere?'

Cautiously Farrah picked up his sword. 'She was heading towards Count Grendel's Castle then.'

'What?'

Zadek nodded. 'I'm afraid it looks as if your friend may have fallen into the hands of the Count.'

The Doctor headed for the door. 'Then I must get her out of there.'

Zadek moved to bar his way. 'Wait, Doctor. We still need your help.' His hand was on his sword-hilt. Farrah too was poised, ready to attack. Persuasively, Zadek went on. 'Castle Gracht is almost impregnable, and Count Grendel is a cruel and ruthless foe. Try to rescue your friend alone, and he will kill you—and her as well. But it you help Prince Reynart to gain the throne, you will have the aid of the King of Tara in your task. The only way you can help your friend, is by helping us.'

47

Romana awoke to find herself still on the same couch, still with Count Grendel and Madame Lamia looking down at her.

'The lovely lady awakens,' murmured Count Grendel.

'How long have I been unconscious?'

'Twelve hours, my dear. I trust you slept well? Release her, Lamia.'

Madame Lamia touched a control and the restraining clamps slid back.

Romana was horrified. 'Twelve hours? Oh no!'

Count Grendel helped her to sit up. 'Why, whatever's the matter, my dear?'

'Look, please let me go,' said Romana desperately. 'I'm no possible use to you, I've got no money, and I'm not even from Tara, so there's no one to ransom me ...'

'Ransom you?' Count Grendel seemed shocked. 'Surely you don't think I'm just a common bandit?'

'I don't know. If you're not a bandit, why kidnap me? What use can I be to you.'

'Come with me, my dear, and I'll show you.'

Romana let Count Grendel help her to her feet. She still felt a little shaky, but she could walk well enough.

'This way,' said Count Grendel. 'There's something I want to show you. Come, Lamia.'

They led Romana away, out of the chamber, through stone-flagged corridors and down a flight of steps. They came to a narrow passage at the end of which was two cell doors. A burly soldier stood on guard, raising his

48

sword in salute as Count Grendel approached.

Count Grendel acknowledged the salute with a casual nod. 'How is our guest, Sergeant Kurster?'

'Well enough, my lord.'

Grendel moved to the peephole set into the cell door. 'Let's see for ourselves.' He glanced through the peephole and then beckoned for Romana. 'Take a look, my dear.'

Romana peered into the cell. It was a bare, stone-walled dungeon. Some attempt had been made to make it more comfortable. There were rugs, a table and some chairs.

An ornately gowned young woman sat by the barred window, busy on a large tapestry-frame. As Romana watched she gave a sigh of boredom, and raised her head.

Romana gave a gasp of astonishment.

She was looking at herself.

5

The Prisoner of Gracht

On closer study, Romana realised that the girl in the cell wasn't *exactly* like her. The hair was a little darker, the nose a fraction longer, the forehead not quite so high. But it was certainly an astonishing resemblance, one that would have deceived anyone but the closest friend or relative.

She looked at the Count. 'It's incredible.'

Count Grendel gave a smile of satisfaction. 'Yes, the resemblance is extraordinary, isn't it?'

'Is she an android?'

'Good Heavens no, my dear. She is Princess Strella, first lady of Tara. A direct descendant of the Royal House, Mistress of the domains of Thervalde, Moretegarde and Freya.' Count Grendel smiled. 'In fact, the most eligible young lady on Tara. Shortly to become, in fairly rapid succession, my fiancée, my bride and then my much-lamented late wife.' He sighed. 'It will be a most tragic accident, a lovely flower cut off in her prime. Naturally, as her widowed husband, I shall claim her estates, her wealth and her position as second in line to the throne—all strictly according to the Laws of Tara. In short, my marriage will reinforce my claim to the throne, and my widowhood will give me the wealth to make sure I keep it.'

Romana was horrified by the ruthlessness of Grendel's schemes. But was puzzled too. 'You've already got a Princess. What do you need me for?'

'In case of accidents, my dear. The Princess does not entirely agree with my plan.'

'I'm not surprised!'

Count Grendel shook his head, as if unable to understand such unreasonable obstinacy. 'In fact, between you and me, she quite refuses to co-operate. She actually says she'd sooner die than marry me.'

'Good for her! I still don't see what all this has got to do with me.'

'Don't you, my dear? I'd have thought that was obvious. If the Princess goes on refusing, and if, sadly, something should happen to her ... I can marry you instead—in front of the assembled nobles of Tara, who won't know the difference.'

'What happens if I refuse too?'

Count Grendel gave his sinisterly charming smile. 'Ah, but you won't, my dear. I can be *very* persuasive. Aren't I a lucky man to have a choice of two such beautiful women for my bride?'

Madame Lamia gave a little hiss of anger.

Romana said, 'Apparently some of your household staff don't agree.'

Count Grendel said carelessly. 'I'm afraid Madame Lamia is prejudiced, my dear. Just because I once showed her a certain courtesy, she had hopes of becoming my Countess.' He sighed. 'That's the trouble with peasants these days, they don't know their place any more.'

Romana couldn't help feeling sorry for Madame Lamia who was burning with anger, but clearly too terrified to speak.

The Count moved across to the second cell door. 'Open up, Kurster.'

The massive sergeant unlocked the door, and threw it open. This cell was just a cell, and nothing more, the only furnishing a filthy straw mattress. A man lay on the mattress and Romana saw with horror that there was a metal collar around his neck. The collar was fastened by a length of chain to an iron ring set in the cell wall. The man wore boots and trousers, and the tattered remains of a once magnificent silk shirt. One arm was in a sling, his face was white, and his eyes burned feverishly. He raised himself on one elbow as the cell door opened. 'Come to gloat, Grendel? Why don't you just kill me and get it over with?'

'I never rush my pleasures, my dear Reynart,' said Count Grendel suavely. 'I've brought someone to see you.' He turned to Romana. 'Allow me to present His Royal Highness, Prince Reynart, first in line to the throne of Tara.'

At the sight of Romana's face the captive leaned forward eagerly. 'Strella!'

Romana shook her head. 'No, I'm sorry. I just happen to look like her. My name's Romana.'

Count Grendel smiled at his prisoner's confusion.

'You see, my dear Reynart, when I play for high stakes I like to hold *all* the cards.'

Romana pushed past him, and knelt beside the man on the bed. She took hold of his wrist, and felt his pulse. 'Well, you won't hold this one much longer, if you're not careful. He's running a fever.'

'That's why we brought him a permanent nurse for his bedside.'

Romana looked round. 'Oh, yes? Who's that then?'

'You, my dear!' Count Grendel's voice hardened. 'Hold her, Kurster. Lamia the collar.'

Before Romana could move, the massive guard seized her above the elbows. Madame Lamia produced a second neck ring from a corner of the cell. It too was linked to a ring in the cell wall by a length of chain.

Romana struggled wildly, but the guard's grip was firm.

'Let her go,' shouted Prince Reynart.

Count Grendel shoved him back on the bed. 'Don't be so tediously heroic, there's a good fellow.'

Lamia slipped the collar around Romana's neck.

Count Grendel looked on in amusement. 'Not too tight, Lamia. We don't want to choke her, do we?'

Lamia fastened the collar and stepped back. 'She is secure, my lord.'

The guard let go of Romana's arms, and went back to the door. 'Splendid,' said Count Grendel affably. 'You really ought to thank me you know, Reynart!'

'For what?'

'For finding you such a charming nurse. Guard our

guests well, Kurster. Watch them constantly.'

'Yes, my lord.'

Count Grendel ushered Lamia out, and paused in the cell doorway for a last look at the Prince. 'And now, my friend, I must leave for your Coronation. Such a pity you won't be there!'

The cell door clanged shut behind him.

'How far away is Count Grendel's castle?' demanded the Doctor.

'About eight leagues due west,' said Zadek. 'Why do you ask, Doctor? You're not still thinking of going there? Even if your friend is Grendel's prisoner we can't be sure that he's holding her at the castle.'

'Where else might he have taken her?'

'To the city of Tara itself, perhaps. He's bound to be there for the Coronation—he'll want to make sure no one else claims the throne.'

The Doctor considered. 'K9 you take the castle, I'll go to Tara with George and our two friends here.'

'You're still going to help us then, Doctor?' asked Zadek.

'It looks like it. If Romana is in Tara she'll probably be somewhere in the Palace—and you're the only one who can get me in there, right?'

'That is correct.'

The Doctor turned to K9. 'All I want *you* to do is to find out whether or not Romana is in the castle. As soon you've done that, report back to me, understood?'

'Understood, Master.'

'Off you go then!'

The Doctor opened the door, and K9 glided out of the hunting lodge.

'Is he a good hunting dog?' asked Farrah curiously.

'He'll find her, if she's there.'

'You wouldn't be interested in selling him?'

'Why don't you ask K9 about it, when he gets back?' suggested the Doctor.

Farrah rubbed his still-tingling hand. 'No, thank you, Doctor, I don't think I will!'

'It's time we were leaving,' said Zadek impatiently. 'The horses, Farrah.'

The Doctor turned to the android, which had been sitting motionless in its chair all this while. 'Come along, Your Royal Highness.'

The android Prince rose, and walked stiffly from the room.

An hours hard ride brought them to the edge of the dense wood that surrounded the Palace of Tara. They left the horses in the charge of one of Prince Reynart's men, continued their journey on foot.

Zadek led them to the crest of a wooded rise and pointed downwards. 'There you are, Doctor. The Palace.'

The Doctor looked at the enormous white building below them, its innumerable towers and turrets crowded inside an encircling wall. Flags were flying, guards patrolled the ramparts and an endless line of people on horseback and on foot, wound its way through the main gates.

'There can't be much time left,' said Zadek. 'Wait here, I'll go and find the tunnel entrance.'

'Be careful, Swordmaster,' said Farrah.

Zadek nodded and slipped away through the trees.

'He's not so young as he was,' Farrah seemed almost ashamed of showing concern.

The Doctor smiled. 'I shouldn't worry about him. I imagine he's still more than capable of taking care of himself.'

Farrah was in a worrying mood. 'What about the android? Do you think the journey might have damaged him?' He turned to the android Prince who stood motionless beside the Doctor. 'Are you all right? How do you feel?'

The android made no reply.

Farrah looked worriedly at the Doctor. 'Is he all right?'

'I think so.'

'Why isn't he talking?'

'I've switched off his speech-circuit to conserve energy.'

Farrah nodded. 'It's a funny thing, but there's something about androids ... I know it's silly, but somehow they make me uneasy. You know what I mean ...'

The Doctor nodded. 'A lot of people feel that way about androids. Mind you, a lot of androids feel that way about people!'

Suddenly Zadek reappeared. 'I've found the tunnel entrance, but it's guarded. This way.'

He led them through the trees, halting them behind a large clump of bushes. 'Look!'

The Doctor and Farrah peered around the bush and saw what looked like the entrance to a small cave. It was guarded by a black-clad figure carrying a crossbow.

'One of Grendel's men,' whispered Zadek. 'It seems the Count knew about the tunnel after all.'

'I'll deal with him,' said Farrah confidently. He adjusted a switch on his sword-hilt and slipped away.

Bored, the guard marched up and down before the cave mouth. He heard a rustling in the bushes to his left and suddenly became alert, raising his crossbow.

He moved cautiously in the direction of the sound.

Suddenly he heard another sound, from behind him this time. The guard swung round and saw a tall young man with a sword in his hand.

It was the last thing he saw. Farrah lunged forwards, and as his sword tip touched the guard's tunic the man's body glowed with a colossal energy-charge, and dropped to the ground. As he fell, his dying hand triggered the loaded crossbow and a tree close by exploded in smoke and flame.

Zadek hurried forward, the Doctor and the android Prince close behind him.

'A crossbow that fires electronic bolts,' said the Doctor. 'Fascinating!'

'A peasants weapon,' said Farrah dismissively.

Zadek was already at the cave mouth. 'Hurry, there isn't much time.'

They followed him into the blackness of the cave.

The android Prince was on his way to his Coronation.

6

The Android King

K9 followed the direction Zadek had indicated, doing his best to keep out of sight on the way. Luckily, the countryside was deserted; everyone had gone to the Palace of Tara for the Coronation.

K9 could move surprisingly quickly when he had to, and before long the towers of Castle Gracht came into sight. Deciding to avoid the main gate, he swung round in a wide circle and approached the castle from the rear. A narrow winding track led him to the edge of a broad, flat stretch of water—the moat was barring his way. K9 considered. He had a surprising range of abilities, but swimming wasn't one of them. K9 stood motionless for a moment, eyes glowing, antennae quivering, his whole body throbbing with power. He revolved first left and then right, sweeping the entire castle with the ray. Suddenly he stopped. The throbbing died down and K9 gave a brief electronic gurgle of satisfaction. He had found what he was looking for— the distinctive alpha wave pattern of Romana's brain-waves. The trace was faint, muffled by the thick stone walls, but it was there. Romana was somewhere inside Castle Gracht.

K9 spun round and moved away.

Madame Lamia was in her android surgery, studying the oddly shaped crystal that had been taken from Count Grendel's latest prisoner.

She scratched at the crystal with a steel scalpel. Nothing happened; the scalpel was unable to make the slightest mark.

Madame Lamia fitted the crystal into a holding clamp and attacked it with a high-speed electric drill. The drill-bit shattered. The crystal was still unmarked.

Lamia sat regarding the crystal with a baffled frown. 'Curious ... very curious.' She had a feeling the crystal was something very important indeed—if only she could discover what it was ...

In the dungeon below, Romana was examining Prince Reynart's wound. It had been made by an electrosword, and it was ugly and inflamed. She restrapped the rough dressing, trying to make him a little more comfortable.

Prince Reynart winced. 'How is it? Bad, eh?' He was pale and shivering, and his eyes glinted feverishly.

'It's not good,' admitted Romana. 'And in a place like this ... How did it happen?'

'I came to, just as they were bringing me into the castle, and tried to escape. One of Grendel's men ran me through.'

Romana settled him back on his mattress. 'Look, don't try to talk. Save your strength.'

'Save it for what?'

'Escape, of course.'

Prince Reynart rubbed his injured shoulder. 'I'm not going to be able to take on Grendel's guards with this, am I? Let alone swim the moat.'

'Don't worry,' said Romana confidently. 'The Doctor will get us out of here.'

'How? No one's ever escaped from Castle Gracht.'

'The Doctor will find a way.'

'Soon, I hope,' gasped Prince Reynart. 'I'd hate to give Grendel the pleasure of seeing me die in his blasted dungeon.'

Sword in hand, Zadek led the Doctor and the android Prince along a gloomy echoing tunnel. Farrah brought up the rear, alert for trouble.

The Doctor looked curiously at the tunnel walls. They were dank and dripping, but obviously man-made, lined with blocks of stone. 'What were these tunnels built for, originally?'

'Plague,' said Zadek briefly.

'What?'

'They were plague tunnels, built about two hundred years ago. They allowed the Royal court to move in and out of the palace without passing through the contaminated city. The great plague wiped out nine tenths of Tara's population.'

The Doctor nodded, thinking that this accounted for the curiously deserted feeling of Tara. The green and fertile planet had only the smallest of populations. 'I suppose that's why you developed the science of building androids—to replace the missing people?'

Farrah nodded. 'They work in the factories and the mines, till the fields. There's still a good deal of prejudice against them though. The noble families won't even have them as servants.'

The Doctor nodded understandingly. 'How much further, Zadek?'

'Quite a way. We'd better hurry.'

When a squad of ten of Count Grendel's men came to reinforce the guard on duty at the tunnel entrance, he was nowhere to be seen. A rapid search revealed his body, thrust into the centre of a bush.

The guards took their crossbows from their shoulders, and hurried into the tunnel.

Gorgeous in their elaborate ceremonial dress the nobility of Tara were waiting outside the double doors that led to the throne room.

The men wore colourful military uniforms, stiff with gold braid, sparkling with medals, the women wore court dresses and their finest jewels.

Count Grendel of Gracht stood a little apart from the rest, studying the Great Clock of Tara which dominated the ante-chamber. Elaborately decorated, its face covered with complex astrological symbols, the Great

Clock was hundreds of years old, but still accurate to a micro-second. A jewelled marker on the rim of the clock face indicated the precise moment at which the new King of Tara must be crowned. The big hand of the clock was very close to the marker now. It quivered and moved a division nearer. Count Grendel smiled.

Incongruous in plain black livery, the giant form of Sergeant Kurster made his way to his master's side. 'Everything is ready, my Lord.'

'The—peasants are prepared?'

'Mercenaries, dressed as peasants are posted at strategic points. As soon as it is announced that Prince Reynart has not appeared for the Coronation, they will lead a spontaneous demonstration of love and loyalty to the House of Gracht.'

'And the Palace Guard?'

'They have been taken care of.'

'I think I shall reject the crown only once,' mused Count Grendel. 'Rejecting it twice might be going too far. Besides, I'm not sure I can trust the Archimandrite to offer it to me a third time!'

Impressive in his high crowned hat and gold-brocaded robes, the Archimandrite of Tara was sweeping towards them. A saintly-looking white-haired old man, he was head of the Church of Tara, and the leading religious figure on the planet. He was also a tough and wily old politician, with a strongly developed sense of survival.

Kurster faded discreetly into the background, and Count Grendel bowed. 'My Lord Archimandrite.'

The Archimandrite looked at the Great Clock. By now the big hand had moved several divisions closer to the marker. 'The hour approaches, Count Grendel.'

'It does indeed, Your Eminence.'

'But where is the Prince?'

'I am sure he will make every effort to be here.'

'If he misses the appointed hour of his Coronation, we must chose another king from the nobles assembled. That is the law,' said the old man fussily.

Count Grendel smiled again. 'I know!'

The Archimandrite looked hard at him. 'In view of the strange absence of Prince Reynart, and the even stranger disappearance of the Princess Strella, your own claim would appear to be the strongest, Count Grendel.'

Count Grendel bowed. 'You overwhelm me, Your Eminence.'

Zadek led his little party towards a sharp right-hand bend in the tunnel. 'The steps leading up to the Coronation Chamber are just around here.'

Suddenly, there was a shout from behind them, and a chunk of masonry close to the Doctor's head exploded in smoke and flame.

They turned, and saw a group of men running towards them down the tunnel. More electronic crossbow bolts flashed past them, exploding against the tunnel walls. They sprang round the corner out of sight. Footsteps rang along the tunnel, coming closer.

Zadek drew his sword. 'Doctor, take the Prince and

make for the steps. We'll ambush them here.'

The Doctor turned and saw that the tunnel ended a few yards further on in a steep flight of steps. He led the Prince towards them.

Farrah and Zadek waited, swords in their hands.

The guards hurled round the corner in a tightly packed group. Zadek and Farrah sprang and the tunnel echoed with the screams of dying men and the crackle of electro-swords. Four of the guards died before they realised what was happening, and the rest found themselves fighting for their lives. There were half a dozen guards left on their feet after that first savage attack, all tough, experienced fighters. The range was too close for crossbow work now. They drew their swords and pressed forward to the attack.

Shoulder to shoulder, Zadek and Farrah stood them off, electro-swords flashing in the darkness. Luckily, the tunnel was only wide enough for their opponents to attack them two at a time. Zadek was a Swordsmaster, Farrah a ranking Swordman, and their fighting skills were far above those of their opponents. But they were still outnumbered three to one, and there was always the danger that one of the guards in the rear would press close enough to slip home a killing stroke.

Zadek disposed of his opponent with relative ease. As the man fell, he yelled, 'There's a lever at the top of the steps Doctor, to your left. Pull it down. It opens a panel.'

Farrah's man fell, and two more guards moved forward to the attack.

Standing the android Prince aside, the Doctor

groped till he found the lever and heaved. It wouldn't move. 'It's stuck!' he yelled. 'When was it last used, two hundred years ago?'

Zadek thrust low, and another of Grendel's guards screamed and died. 'Try again, Doctor,' he yelled. 'We must get through!'

The Doctor's voice floated back. 'It's no good—it won't budge ...'

A savage slash from Farrah disposed of his opponent. Only two guards left now.

Zadek and Farrah fell back, pretending weariness, luring their last two opponents to the foot of the steps.

The Doctor heaved desperately on the lever—and it shifted. Only an inch or two ... but it moved!

Taking a deep breath the Doctor heaved again. 'It's coming!'

Swords flashing, Farrah and Zadek sprang forward ...

One more time-division and the big hand of the Great Clock would touch the jewelled marker.

'There is no sign of the Prince, Count Grendel,' said the Archimandrite worriedly.

'He would appear to be late,' agreed Count Grendel sadly.

'If he does not appear at the appointed time, it is my duty to offer the crown to one of the other nobles. As I said, your claim is a strong one. But there are other claimants ...'

Count Grendel smiled. 'The decision is yours, and

yours alone, my dear Archimandrite. But you may rest assured that you yourself, and whoever you choose to be King of Tara will immediately be offered the full protection of my guards.'

'*Your* guards?' The Archimandrite glanced round. Black uniformed men were filing through the door, taking up strategic positions all round the room. 'These are *your men*?'

'The Palace Guard was—indisposed. I thought it only right to offer my help.'

The Archimandrite looked shrewdly at him. 'Perhaps it would be simpler if I offered you the crown now!'

'Good heavens no, my dear Archimandrite. We must wait for the exact moment. Everything must be done correctly.'

'Noble sentiments Count Grendel, and nobly spoken,' said the old man drily. 'But look—it *is* time!'

The big hand quivered, jerked forward and touched the jewelled marker—closing an electronic circuit.

There was a fanfare of trumpets, and the double doors to the Coronation Room swung open.

Beyond them was a long, high-ceilinged hall, sunlight streaming through stained glass windows, shining on ancient faded tapestries. At the far end of the hall short wide steps led up to a raised dais.

On the dais was a throne—and on the throne sat Prince Reynart, orb and sceptre already in his hands.

Zadek and Farrah stood one each side of the throne, the Doctor was behind it.

67

'Impossible!' hissed Grendel.

The Archimandrite seized his moment. He had never cared much for Count Grendel, and he knew that despite the presence of his guards, even the Count would not dare to flout tradition completely.

The Archimandrite strode forward, leading the assembled nobles into the Coronation Room.

When all were in position, he called. 'Kneel! All kneel to Prince Reynart, soon to be King of Tara.'

The assembled nobles of Tara knelt. All except Count Grendel, who stood glaring incredulously at the figure on the throne. 'Kneel!' ordered the Archimandrite.

Reluctantly, Grendel knelt.

On a stand before the throne was a velvet cushion, bearing a golden crown. The Archimandrite went over and lifted the crown, holding it high above Reynart's head. 'Behold the Crown of Tara!'

Prince Reynart lurched forward a fraction in his chair.

Farrah and Zadek exchanged agonised glances.

The Doctor held his breath.

The android Prince stopped moving.

The Archimandrite placed the crown on Prince Reynart's head. 'Hail to the King! Hail to King Reynart of Tara!'

There was another flourish of electronic trumpets.

The chant crashed back from the crowd. 'Hail! Hail to the King!'

There was a sudden silence. The Archimandrite

leaned forward, and whispered, 'Your Majesty, the speech of accession! You must give the speech or the ceremony is not complete.'

King Reynart sat silent and motionless.

The Doctor held his breath, wondering if the recently repaired speech circuits would respond with the programmed words.

From the back of the hall, Count Grendel stared hard at the silent King.

Suddenly, King Reynart spoke. 'My subjects ... I acknowledge your salutations, and swear that I will uphold your rights and devote myself to defending and protecting you at all times.' His voice was a little faint, but quite distinct.

The Doctor gave a great sigh of relief, and leaned closer to Zadek. 'I must do a bit more work on his speech circuits,' he whispered.

The Archimandrite raised his voice again. 'Let all nobles now swear the oath of fealty to the King, according to rank and precedence. Let the first lady of Tara come forward.'

A plump and matronly Grand Duchess was about to move forward, when a slender gowned figure slipped past her and mounted the steps.

Count Grendel backed away.

There was a murmur of astonishment from the crowd—and no one was more surprised than the Doctor. 'It's Romana!'

Zadek shook his head. 'It's the Princess Strella,' he whispered. 'The one who disappeared.'

Princess Strella said, 'I, Princess Strella, descendant of the High Kings of Tara, Mistress of the domains of Thorvald, Mortgarde and Freya, do humbly offer my loyalty to His Majesty King Reynart, and do hereby recognise his sovereignity.' She knelt, as if to kiss the King's hand.

'No!' shouted the Doctor suddenly. Snatching the heavy sceptre from the King, he smashed it down with savage force on the kneeling girl's head.

7

Invitation to an Ambush

There were shrieks of astonished horror, shouts of anger. Several noblemen leaped forward, swords in their hands.

'Seize him,' quavered the shocked Archimandrite. 'He has killed Princess Strella!'

'No,' shouted Farrah. 'That is not the Princess. Look!'

The face-mask of the fallen figure had been smashed away, revealing a maze of electronic circuitry inside the skull.

'It's an android,' whispered the Archimandrite.

Zadek moved close to the Doctor. 'How did you know?'

'There must have been a minute circuit-defect. I heard it sparking.'

'It doesn't make sense,' the Archimandrite was protesting. 'Why send an android to swear loyalty to the King?'

The Doctor came forward. 'To get close enough to kill him!'

Count Grendel shoved his way to the front of the crowd and glared furiously at the Doctor. He remem-

bered seeing this extraordinary-looking fellow unconscious on the floor with the others, the night they'd
kidnapped the Prince from the hunting lodge. Count
Grendel had assumed he was some mountebank friend
of Prince Reynart, and left him with the others. It
was galling to think he could have killed him then
with ease—instead of leaving him alive to spoil his
plans.

The Archimandrite said, 'But who would wish to
kill the King. Unless—some rival claimant to the
throne ...' He turned and looked at Count Grendel,
who said smoothly, 'My dear Archimandrite, what
ever are you suggesting?'

'Isn't that obvious,' snapped Zadek. 'Treachery!
Treachery to the King!'

'Take care what you say, Zadek,' snarled Count
Grendel. Calming himself, he turned to the Archimandrite. 'Your Eminence, may I suggest that we
postpone the rest of the oath-taking ceremony? Who
knows how many other programmed androids there
may be?'

The old Archimandrite was horrified. 'You think
there are more of these things?'

'It is a possibility we must face, Your Eminence. I
shall leave my personal guards here to protect the
King.'

Zadek drew himself upright. 'I am afraid I cannot
permit that, Count Grendel.'

'The decision is not yours, Zadek,' said Count Grendel furiously.

Zadek met his angry gaze, quite unafraid. 'I command His Majesty's bodyguard. The decision is mine and mine alone.'

Suddenly, Count Grendel was looking at the King. 'You presume too much, Swordmaster Zadek. What does His Majesty have to say on the subject? He is very silent.'

'His Majesty is tired, and suffering from the strain of the occasion,' said the Doctor hurriedly. 'Why don't we discuss this matter later?'

'Who the devil are you, sir?' demanded Count Grendel angrily.

'I am the Royal Physician,' said the Doctor with immense dignity. 'You can call me Doctor.'

'Is His Majesty ill?' asked the Archimandrite worriedly.

'Oh, no, no! Nothing that a little rest won't cure. He'll be fine by tomorrow.'

The Archimandrite looked hard at him. 'I understand Doctor. Come, Count Grendel, we must leave His Majesty to rest.'

'But what of the danger?' protested Grendel.

The Doctor said, 'There can be no danger, when the King has his own personal staff to protect him. Can there, Count Grendel?'

With a snarl, Grendel turned away.

The Archimandrite led the Court from the chamber, and the other nobles followed them.

As the doors swung closed, Zadek gave a sigh of relief. He looked worriedly at King Reynart—still sitting a little lopsidedly on his throne. '*Will* he be all right tomorrow, Doctor?'

'Not unless I recharge his power pack and repair his speech circuits.'

Farrah looked down at the faceless figure on the steps. 'It's a good job you realised she was an android.'

'Well, I knew it wasn't Romana. And when I heard the sparking and saw Grendel start to back away—I guessed he was using one of his contingency plans.' The Doctor sighed. 'I wish I knew for sure where the real Romana was ... And what's happened to K9?'

Romana sat watching over Prince Reynart, who was dozing fitfully on his straw mattress, tossing and turning, and muttering in his sleep.

Abruptly, the cell door was flung open with a crash and two guards marched in. One unlocked Romana's chain from the wall-ring, the other pulled her roughly to her feet.

Prince Reynart awoke with a start and shouted, 'Let her go, peasants! You have no right to lay hands on a lady!' He struggled to get up, but one of the guards shoved him brutally back on to the mattress. Reynart collapsed, muttering deliriously, and the guards marched Romana from the cell.

They took her back to the android surgery, where Madame Lamia was studying the crystal. She held it up as Romana was thrust into the room. 'This is yours, I believe?'

'Yes.'

'What is it? What is it made of?'

'I've no idea. I found it near the castle the other day.'

'You're sure of that? It's not like an substance I've ever heard of round here. I've broken two diamond-tipped drills on it.'

'Perhaps it's some kind of quartz,' said Romana casually. 'May I have it back? I mean you don't want it do you, it's no use to you.'

She held out her hand.

Madame Lamia shrugged. 'I suppose not . . .' she was actually about to hand the crystal over, then changed her mind. 'I think I'll keep it for a while.'

'Whatever for?'

'I'm curious . . . I have the strangest feeling that it's part of something . . . something very important.'

The crystal was part of the Key to Time—one of the most important objects in the cosmos, but Romana had no intention of telling Madame Lamia *that*.

There was shouting and cursing in the corridor outside, the clatter of booted feet, and Count Grendel burst into the room, his faithful dwarf Till at his heels.

Count Grendel was tired, travel stained and in a terrible temper. He snatched off his riding cloak and hurled it at Till, almost burying the little man in its folds.

'It failed, Lamia!' he bawled. 'Your precious machine failed. That Doctor saw at once that it was an android.'

75

'The Doctor——' began Romana. She stopped herself quickly. Apparently the Doctor was alive and well and giving Count Grendel trouble. Perhaps it wouldn't be wise to reveal she'd come to Tara as his companion.

'My Lord, I did warn you that it wasn't yet ready for use,' protested Lamia. 'Who is this Doctor you speak of?'

'Some strange fellow who seems to be assisting the Prince,' growled Grendel. His eyes were on Romana's face. 'You know this Doctor, I think?'

'Never heard of him,' said Romana innocently.

Count Grendel smiled cruelly. 'I think you do ... Lamia you will prepare another android, an exact copy of our guest here, precise to the last detail. I think she can help us to dispose of this Doctor.'

He nodded to the guards. They seized Romana and dragged her towards the couch.

The King of Tara sat on a high-backed chair in one of the rooms of the Royal Suite, while the Doctor made precise adjustments to the circuitry of his brain.

There was a noise in the corridor and Zadek hurried in. 'That robot dog of yours is back, Doctor. Caused quite a commotion at the palace gates.'

K9 glided into the room and announced importantly. 'I have found Mistress Romana. She is in the Castle of Gracht.'

The Doctor looked up eagerly. 'You're sure, K9?'

'Affirmative Master. I detected her brain-wave pattern quite distinctly.'

'Good dog!' The Doctor looked at Zadek. 'That means the Count now has Romana, the real Prince and probably the real Princess as well.'

'So Grendel holds all the cards!'

The Doctor nodded towards the figure in the chair. 'Not *all* of them. We still have a King ourselves—of a sort.'

'Our King has shortly to attend an important meeting with the Archimandrite and the College of Priests,' said Zadek grimly. 'Will he be able to manage it?'

The Doctor rubbed his chin. 'K9, if I patched the carbon and silicon circuits together, how long would the linkage hold?'

'Three hours, nine minutes, and ten point seven seconds,' replied K9 promptly.

'Better than I thought! I think I can promise you, Zadek, King George will acquit himself right loyally with the Priesthood—just as long as the meeting doesn't go on too long.'

'And if it does?'

The Doctor gave a rueful grin. 'If it does, there'll be a blue flash, a lot of smoke, and a nasty smell of burning plastic...'

Romana was strapped to the couch again, and Madame Lamia was passing a hand-scanner above her face and body, feeding the precise contours into a computer so that she could reproduce them in android form.

When the scan was finished, Lamia went over to the computer read-out screen to study the results.

Count Grendel was looking on. He smiled benignly down at Romana. 'Comfortable, my dear?'

Romana scowled up at him, and said nothing.

'My lord?' called Lamia excitedly.

'Well?'

'There are some very unusual readings here! The alpha waves are like nothing I have seen before. This girl is not from Tara.'

'From where, then?' asked Grendel lazily. 'What is she?'

'I cannot tell. I need more time for evaluations.'

The Count rose and stretched. 'Time is something we do not have, my dear. Just programme another android to kill—and make sure it's a perfect copy. The Doctor is not an easy man to deceive.'

Romana stared up at him in horror. Her android double was to be used to kill the Doctor.

The android King sat upright in his chair. He had just been programmed for the coming meeting with the Archimandrite, and Zadek was anxiously testing the results of the Doctor's briefing.

'The question of monastic lands is bound to come up. What is your Majesty's position on the matter?'

The King turned to look at him. 'Monastic lands are held by religious orders only under the protection of the crown—which can be withdrawn at any time. However, I propose to continue that protection—subject of course to the loyal support of my Priesthood—

78

and adequate contributions to the Royal funds.'

Zadek shook his head wonderingly. 'Excellent! You know Doctor, I sometimes think that the Prince here——'

'King!' said the figure at the table firmly.

'I beg your pardon Your Majesty——' Zadek broke off. 'You know, I keep forgetting he's only an android. Trouble is, Doctor the King seems to be ... how shall I put it, a trifle more ...'

The Doctor grinned. 'More intelligent than the real one? Well, of course he is. I programmed him.'

Zadek lowered his voice. 'Well, don't make him too intelligent Doctor. You can't really trust androids you know.'

'A lot of androids I know say that about humans,' said the Doctor solemnly. 'Don't worry, Zadek. Why be afraid of something that goes bang when it gets a short-circuit?'

Farrah marched into the room. 'A visitor for the Doctor.'

Zadek frowned. 'Who is it?'

A squat broad-shouldered figure thrust its way past Farrah and came into the room. 'My name is Till, bodyservant to Count Grendel.'

Zadek looked suspiciously at him. 'And what do you want here?'

'My mission is with the Doctor, not with you— Swordmaster.' The little man's voice turned the title into an insult.

Touchy as ever, Farrah reached for his sword, 'How

dare you speak thus to a Master of the Sword, you miserable lout!'

Till was unmoved. 'I speak only with the Doctor, Swordsman. Those are my orders.'

The Doctor stood up. 'Quite right too, we peasants must stick together. 'He took Till by the arm and led him to the far end of the room. 'Now, what can I do for you?'

Till lowered his voice. 'I bear a message from Madame Lamia.'

'And who might she be?'

'She is Count Grendel's woman. A peasant, like me.'

'Well?'

'Madame Lamia fears for the Count's safety. Now that your android has been crowned King, Count Grendel's political power is slipping away ... she fears he will fail, be captured and executed ...' Till lowered his voice still further.

At the other end of the room Zadek and Farrah listened hard, but they could hear no more than a low rumble.

'He *can* be trusted, I suppose?' muttered Farrah.

'Who? Grendel's servant?'

'No. the Doctor.'

'I hope so,' said Zadek. 'We know very little about him.'

Farrah looked at the two figures at the other end of the room. They were still talking in low, urgent voices.

'I don't like it,' said Farrah suddenly. 'I'm going to put a stop to this.'

His hand went to his sword.

K9 swung round to cover him. 'Do not activate that sword ...'

Farrah took his hand away from his sword-hilt. 'Good dog,' he said uneasily. 'Good dog.'

Till nodded to the Doctor and strode out of the room, ignoring the others. The Doctor came over to them. 'Madame Lamia is offering us a deal.'

'You refused, of course.'

'No, I accepted,' said the Doctor cheerfully. 'I've got to take a written guarantee signed by you, Zadek, on behalf of the King, that Count Grendel won't be harmed. In return, Madame Lamia and her friends will hand Romana, the Prince and the Princess over to me. She wants me to meet her, tonight. Says she'll release Romana first, as a gesture of good faith.'

'It's a trap,' said Farrah. 'You can't possibly go.'

'Of course it's a trap—and of course I'm going! If they really do bring Romana, I can get her away from them at least.'

Zadek looked dubious. 'And where is this meeting to take place?'

'Somewhere poetically called the Pavilion of The Summer Winds—do you know it?'

Zadek nodded. 'It's a summer house in the woods on Grendel's estate, quite close to the castle. We'd better come with you, Doctor.'

The Doctor shook his head. 'You've got to look after His Majesty. Besides, they want me to go alone. They always want you to go alone, when you're walking into a trap. I wonder what nasty ideas they're cooking up for me?'

The Doctor rose. 'Well, I'll be off. Come on K9. You two take King George here, and a squad of men, and meet me at the hunting lodge. We'll make our next move from there.'

Zadek and Farrah looked at each other. Not only was the Doctor heading straight into danger—he actually seemed to be looking forward to it!

8

The Android Killer

Romana stood in the android surgery, looking wonderingly at a perfect replica of herself. The Count was beside her, obviously delighted with Madame Lamia's work. 'You've excelled yourself, my dear Lamia. It's absolutely perfect.' He turned to Romana, the real Romana. 'Don't you agree, my dear?'

Romana said scornfully. 'The Doctor will spot it immediately.'

Count Grendel laughed. 'In the dark, at a distance of twenty feet? I think not, my dear.'

Romana had a horrid feeling that Grendel was right. 'He'll know it's a trap, anyway.'

'Of course. That's what gives the situation such a delicious edge.'

'Well, if he knows it's a trap, he won't come.'

Grendel stroked his chin. 'You underestimate him, my dear. Of course he'll come. It's his only chance of rescuing you. Oh, he'll be very careful. But sooner or later, he'll have to find out if that figure in the darkened pavilion is you—and when he does ... Show her, Lamia, my dear.'

Lamia went into her workshop and returned carrying a blank faced dummy which she propped up in the corner of the room. She pressed a button in its chest, and jumped hastily back. To Romana's astonishment, the Doctor's voice came from somewhere inside the dummy. 'Hullo, Romana, how are you?'

The android Romana swung round to face the dummy. Light flashed from the buckle in the android's belt—and the dummy exploded.

Count Grendel rubbed his hands. 'Ingenious, don't you think? You really are to be congratulated, Lamia, my dear.'

'How did you get the voice?' asked Romana.

Madame Lamia smiled. 'Till, the Count's servant was carrying a hidden recorder, when he spoke to the Doctor.'

'You've wasted a lot of effort,' said Romana. 'It won't work, you know. Suppose the Doctor doesn't speak?'

'The android is programmed to kill in other ways...'

Count Grendel put his arm around the android Romana. 'You see before you the complete killing machine, my dear. As beautiful as you, and as deadly as the plague itself. If only she were real, I'd marry her!'

'Why don't you do it anyway?' suggested Romana. 'You deserve each other!'

Count Grendel gave the android a courtly bow. 'Come, my dear.' Offering the android his arm, he led it from the room.

Madame Lamia followed them to the door. 'Guard!' she shouted.

Romana backed hastily to the work bench, slipped a steel probe into her sleeve, and moved forward again.

'Guard!' shouted Madame Lamia again.

There was a clatter of booted feet, and a guard came running into the surgery.

Madame Lamia was in a furious temper. 'Why were you so long?' Before the guard could answer she snapped. 'Help me to take this prisoner back to the dungeons.'

The guard marched Romana back to her cell, Lamia following close behind.

In the dungeon the Prince had fallen back into his uneasy sleep. He stirred uneasily, but did not awaken.

Lamia turned to the guard. 'Leave us. I'll lock up the prisoner.'

The guard left the cell, and with vicious satisfaction, Lamia attached Romana's chain to the ring on the cell wall, and snapped home the lock.

Romana looked pityingly at her. 'You know, even if Grendel does become King, he'll never marry you.'

Lamia's voice was shaking with anger. 'Nor you either—I'll see to that!'

'Ah, but I don't want to marry him—and you do! Why don't you just let me go? All you have to do is release me, give me my crystal back, and I'll find the Doctor and leave Tara for ever. Think about it—what have you got to lose?'

'Count Grendel,' said Lamia simply.

'You haven't really got him now, have you? All he's doing is using you.'

'I know. But it's better than nothing.' Lamia turned and left the cell.

When the door had closed behind her, Romana slipped the probe from her sleeve, and began studying the lock on her collar. Basically it was a Taran version of the padlock, and it looked clumsy and old-fashioned. Romana slipped the probe into the keyhole and began probing experimentally. It was difficult—she couldn't see what she was doing. Unfortunately, lock-picking was one of the things they hadn't taught her at the Academy. 'Now, let me see ... how does the Doctor do this?' she muttered.

The Pavilion of the Summer Winds looked peaceful and innocent in the afternoon sunshine. It was a simple wooden summerhouse with a wide verandah, a place for picnics and lazy days in the sun. It was hard to think that it could conceal a deadly ambush.

The Doctor's rendezvous was set for the evening, so he naturally turned up several hours early. He stood at the edge of the little clearing, while K9 scanned the building with his sensor ray.

'Anybody about, K9?'

'Negative, Master.'

'Good. Let's take a look inside.'

There was little enough to see, just one big airy room, furnished with a scattered assortment of old chairs and tables. The shutters were drawn and the room was dark and cool.

The Doctor had a quick look round, while K9 scanned the room for hidden death traps.

'Find anything K9?'

'Negative, Master.'

'Me neither! Well, all we can do now is wait.' Choosing the most comfortable chair, the Doctor sank into it, stretched out his legs and appeared to fall into a doze.

K9 glided to a position in a dark corner and de-activated himself to conserve energy.

They waited.

It infuriated Romana that a graduate of the Academy of Gallifrey should have such difficulty in picking a simple padlock. But she worked on patiently, and at last the lock sprang open. Romana went over to the Prince and shook him gently awake. 'Come on. We're getting out of here. I can open your collar and——'

Feebly the Prince shook his head. 'Save . . . yourself.'

'I won't leave you behind,' whispered Romana fiercely. 'They'll kill you.'

'Too . . . weak. I'd only get in the way.'

'Listen, I think I heard Grendel leaving the castle, a little while ago. It sounded as if he was taking a lot of the guards with him. This could be our chance.'

'Then take it!' The Prince propped himself up on one elbow. 'Don't waste time with me, we'd just both get recaptured. You escape, find my Swordmaster, Zadek, tell him where I am. He'll know what to do.'

Romana hated the idea of leaving the Prince, but she knew he was right. It was the only thing to do. 'All right. But you can still help me.' She explained her plan, and the Prince listened, nodding eagerly.

A few minutes later, Romana began shouting, 'Guard! Guard! Come quickly. The Prince!'

It took a lot of yelling and screaming, but at last the cell door was flung open and a suspicious looking guard stood scowling in the doorway.

'The Prince,' screamed Romana. 'Look he's dying!'

The Prince was writhing to and fro on his mattress, gasping for breath.

'You'd better help him,' said Romana. 'Count Grendel will be furious if the Prince dies while he still needs him.'

The guard came over to the Prince and stood looking down at him. Swiftly Romana slipped out of the cell door slamming it behind her.

The guard spun round. 'Come back!' he yelled. 'Somebody stop her.'

Prince Reynart struggled painfully to his feet, gathered a length of his neck-chain into a loop, and smashed it down on the guard's head. The guard slumped to the floor.

Reynart looked at his chain with great satisfaction. At least he had managed to strike one blow against Count Grendel . . .

As Romana had hoped, most of the guards had left

with Count Grendel, and the corridors of the castle were deserted.

She found her way back to the arched doorway and slipped out into the cobbled courtyard.

She could scarcely believe her luck. The portcullis was raised, the drawbridge down. A bored looking guard stood outside the gatehouse, staring out over the peaceful countryside. And best of all, a ready-saddled horse stood tethered to a ring in the courtyard wall.

Romana knew she had to seize the moment. If the guard turned, if someone else came into the courtyard, the chance would be lost.

She edged along the wall until she reached the horse, and unfastened its reins. Then, trying to remember the way Count Grendel had mounted, she scrambled into the saddle.

The horse, a stolid, well-trained battle charger endured all this quite patiently. Romana shook the reins. 'Come on charger. Go!'

Nothing happened.

Stuck up on the great horse like a statue, Romana felt horribly conspicuous. Someone was bound to see her in a minute. Someone did.

A second guard strolled out of the gatehouse and leaned his back against the wall enjoying the shade. He glanced casually at the horse, then looked again, as he realised with astonishment that there was someone on it.

'Hey!' he bellowed. 'Escaping prisoner!'

The gate guard turned and saw Romana. Both guards ran towards her.

'Oh, go, you stupid creature, *go*,' yelled Romana, and kicked the horse in the ribs. It was a feeble enough kick but it was the signal the horse had been waiting for. It broke into a rapid trot.

Romana kicked again. The trot became a gallop. The horse thundered past the astonished guards, clattered over the drawbridge and galloped away.

The guards ran into the gatehouse, fetched crossbows and fired after the rapidly disappearing figure.

But it was too late. Soon horse and rider had vanished into the forest.

A short time earlier, a ring of Count Grendel's guards was encircling the Pavilion of the Summer Winds, not far away. Sergeant Kurster checked their positions, and reported back to Count Grendel. The Count was waiting with Madame Lamia and the android Romana behind a massive tree opposite the Pavilion entrance.

Kurster saluted. 'The men are in position, my lord ...'

'Good. Now remember, only the Doctor is to be admitted, no one else. Tell the men to await my signals.'

'Yes my lord.' Kurster moved away and Grendel turned to Madame Lamia. 'You know what to do, my dear?'

'Yes. When this Doctor arrives, you can leave him to me.'

'What should I do without you,' said Grendel softly.

Lamia's voice was bitter. 'Find another peasant who understands androids, no doubt.'

Grendel bent and kissed her. 'True. But I should not find one who pleased me so much!' His voice hardened. 'Now go, before the Doctor arrives.'

Madame Lamia crossed the clearing, and went into the pavilion. She stopped in astonishment at the sight of the tall figure in the chair.

'Hullo,' said the Doctor affably. 'You're early!'

Lamia fought to overcome her shock. 'You are the Doctor?'

'That's right.' The Doctor rose and bowed. 'Madame Lamia, I presume.'

'It is not yet time for our meeting . . .'

The Doctor beamed. 'I know, but I had nothing much else to do and it was such a lovely afternoon, I thought I'd come early to enjoy the peace and quiet. What's your story?'

'Do I need one?'

'No, but it might have been fun to hear it. Where's Romana?'

The Doctor's unexpected presence had thrown Madame Lamia off balance. She paused, struggling to regain control. 'You agree to my terms?'

The Doctor produced a sheet of parchment from his pocket. 'A guarantee of safety for Grendel—in return for Romana, now, the Prince and Princess later, all unharmed.' He returned the paper to his pocket. 'You realise the Count will have to live in exile somewhere? But of course, there's no reason why you couldn't go with him, is there?'

Lamia was silent.

'Now,' said the Doctor gently. 'Where's Romana?'

'Outside.'

'Then bring her in.'

Lamia turned and went to the door.

The Doctor's voice halted her at the threshold. 'I don't know if your offer was genuine, Lamia—but my acceptance is.'

Lamia hesitated, turned and went outside.

The Doctor waited, glancing briefly towards the corner where K9 waited, hidden in the shadows.

The door opened and Romana came in, Madame Lamia just behind her.

The Doctor looked at Romana, but did not speak.

'Well, Doctor,' said Lamia nervously. 'Aren't you going to greet your friend?'

There was an alarmed electronic bleep, and K9 glided forward. 'Danger, Master!'

Lamia jumped back. 'Kill the Doctor!' she shouted.

The Doctor flung himself aside as the android Romana's laser-ray blasted a hole in the wall behind him.

'K9!' yelled the Doctor.

Before the android could fire again, K9 had fired his blaster at full strength, blowing the android apart.

Outside the Pavilion, Count Grendel heard the explosion. 'Something's gone wrong. Attack the Pavilion!'

Guards appeared from behind the trees, and began

advancing towards the Pavilion, crossbows at the ready.

'Shoot him down!' shouted Grendel furiously. 'The Doctor must not escape alive!'

9

Flag of Truce

A cloaked figure dashed out of the Pavilion, and the guards raised their crossbows.

'My lord, my lord!' called Madame Lamia desperately.

'Hold your fire!' screamed Grendel.

It was too late. An electronic bolt from the crossbow of a too-eager guard struck Lamia in the heart, and she fell dead to the ground.

'Hold your fire, you fools,' shouted Grendel again. 'That was Madame Lamia!' He looked down at the huddled form for a moment and drew a deep breath. 'Doctor, I know you're in there,' he shouted. 'There's only one entrance to this Pavilion and we have it covered. Come out and parley with me, I promise you won't be harmed.'

Count Grendel lowered his voice. 'Kurster, tell the men to fire at will, as soon as he appears. I want this Doctor *destroyed!*'

In the Pavilion, the Doctor could hear Grendel's voice. 'Well, Doctor, are you coming out? We can still make a deal for the lives of your friends. Come out and talk. I give you my word as a Gracht, you will not be harmed.'

The Doctor looked down. 'Ah well, K9, I suppose I'd better talk to him.'

'Inadvisable, Master.'

'What? Just you leave this to me, K9, I know exactly what I'm doing. Even a villain like Gracht has some sense of honour, and when he swears by his family name . . .'

The Doctor flung open the Pavilion door and popped outside. A volley of crossbow-bolts exploded all around him and he jumped back in, slamming the door behind him. 'I think it's time we were getting out of here, don't you, K9?'

'Affirmative, Master.'

The Doctor studied the Pavilion wall. 'Right! About there, I think!' He pointed.

K9 swung round, raised his head and blasted a sizeable hole through the wall.

'Good dog!' said the Doctor and started through the hole; K9 followed.

Although Grendel had posted men all round the Pavilion, most of them had converged on the front entrance, in response to Grendel's call to attack.

The Doctor and K9 made their way through the hole and headed for the shelter of the trees. At that moment, a guard turned the corner of the Pavilion and spotted them.

'This way! He's over here!' He raised his crossbow

to fire, and K9 promptly blasted him down.

In the front of the Pavilion, Grendel heard the man's dying scream.

'Round the back,' he shouted. 'A thousand gold pieces to the man who shoots the Doctor!'

As the guards ran for the back of the Pavilion there was a thunder of hooves and an enormous charger galloped into the clearing. Grendel looked up at the rider. 'Hold your fire! It's the Princess!' (Count Grendel had no desire for Princess Strella to die *before* he married her.)

The horsewoman galloped around to the rear of the Pavilion. Grendel ran after him, followed by his men.

To his astonished rage he saw the Doctor swinging up into the saddle behind the rider.

'Off you go, K9!' yelled the Doctor. 'Everyone for himself!' The horse galloped away.

'Fools! Dolts!' bellowed Count Grendel. 'That's not the Princess, it's Romana. Get after them!'

The guards began running after the fast-disappearing horse. It was a hopeless task to begin with, and K9 discouraged them still further by shooting down several of the leaders.

The guards turned and fled.

By the time Count Grendel had rallied his demoralised forces, the Doctor, Romana and K9 were all far away.

Zadek's finger jabbed down at the map. 'While Grendel thinks we're still in the palace, there's a chance we can surprise him. If we bring up our men under cover of darkness and position them *here* . . .'

The door to the hunting lodge burst open, and the Doctor and Romana rushed in.

Zadek looked at the Doctor's companion in astonishment. 'Princess Strella!'

'No, I'm Romana. I just look like Strella.'

Romana was equally astonished at the sight of the figure sitting stiffly at the head of the table. 'Prince Reynart!'

'No, that's George,' explained the Doctor hurriedly. 'He's an android.'

'Incredible! And these gentlemen?'

The Doctor grinned. 'Oh, they're real enough—I think!'

Zadek bowed and clicked his heels. 'I am Swordmaster Zadek. This is Swordsman Farrah.'

'Zadek?' said Romana. 'I've got a message for you, from the Prince.'

'You've seen His Majesty?' asked Zadek eagerly.

'He's in the dungeons of Castle Gracht, and he's badly injured. We've got to rescue him.'

Suddenly Farrah went over to the window. 'Horsemen approaching.'

Zadek hurried to join him. 'It's Count Grendel with a flag of truce!'

Farrah's hand went to his sword. 'Shall I kill the traitor, sir?'

Zadek was horrified. 'Under a flag of truce? You

know the Rules of War, Swordsman Farrah.'

Romana looked at the Doctor. 'I'm not sure if Count Grendel does, though.'

'You may be right. Come on.' The Doctor took Romana's arm and led her to the balcony.

'What are you doing, Doctor?'

'Grendel's got no reason to love you, and if he is planning any dirty work I don't want you involved. You just keep out of sight until he's gone.'

Ignoring Romana's protests, the Doctor bustled her out, and rejoined the others. 'Right, then let's see what Grendel wants.'

'Bring in the Count, Swordsman Farrah,' ordered Zadek. 'And make sure you disarm him first!'

Farrah hurried out. A few minutes later he returned, ushering Grendel before him. Farrah was carrying the Count's sword. The Count himself was carrying the traditional white flag, mounted on a long pole with a gilded, ornamental head. Count Grendel bowed, and flourished his flag. 'Good day, gentlemen. I come under a flag of truce, and I expect to be treated according to the usages of war.'

'What do you want?' asked Zadek bluntly.

Grendel turned and looked at the uniformed figure at the head of the table. 'How are you, Your Android Majesty?'

The figure turned its head. 'I ... am ... well.'

Grendel looked maliciously at the Doctor. 'He doesn't sound it, does he? Leakage in the power-cells I expect?'

'Nothing that can't be fixed,' said the Doctor cheerfully.

Count Grendel laughed. 'You know, I like you, Doctor. I was *glad* when you managed to get away safely.'

'So was I!' said the Doctor frankly.

Count Grendel glanced round the room. 'And where is the charming Lady Romana?'

'What do you *want*, Grendel?' interrupted Zadek angrily.

'A private word with the Doctor—according to the Rules of War.'

The Doctor allowed Grendel to lead him to the end of the room. 'Well, Count Grendel?'

'Doctor,' began Grendel, 'You are a remarkable man.'

'Thank you,' said the Doctor modestly.

'Indeed, a man after my own heart.'

The Doctor rubbed his chin. 'I suppose that's meant as a compliment. Go on.'

'Here you are, new to Tara, new to our politics, and in no time at all, what have you become?'

'You tell me.'

'King-maker extraordinary,' said Grendel expansively. He glanced at the uniformed figure, facing them at the end of the table. 'Thanks to your keeping that collection of micro-circuity going, Zadek still has his King. But what would happen if something went seriously wrong in public, like an overload on his circuits? Come to that what would happen to you if Zadek

99

managed to get the real Prince back?'

'What?'

'Your usefulness would cease, Doctor—and you would know too much. You would become a dangerous embarrassment to Zadek, and embarrassment to be got rid of—and don't think he wouldn't do it!'

The Doctor looked curiously at him. 'Count Grendel, exactly what are you suggesting?'

'Suppose we *both* un-made our Kings, eh? No more Reynart at all, alive or android.'

'What would that achieve?'

'A vacancy for a new King!'

The Doctor laughed. 'You, I suppose?'

'No, no, Doctor. Unfortunately, I have enemies. There would be opposition. Far better a stranger, someone above our politics.' Grendel paused. 'I think you would make an excellent King, Doctor—with myself as your chief adviser, of course.'

The Doctor gave a shout of laughter. 'Zadek, Farrah,' he called. 'Count Grendel has just offered me the crown of Tara!'

Zadek was outraged. 'That is treason!'

'Only as long as the King is still alive!' Suddenly Count Grendel drew back his arm and hurled his flag-pole across the room, like a spear. It thudded into the chest of the still figure at the table and the android exploded in a cloud of smoke.

'Seize him,' yelled Zadek.

The Count was already hurtling across the room. With one flying leap, he went through the window in a shower of glass. The Doctor ran after him, and saw Count Grendel leap into the saddle of his waiting horse and ride furiously away. Another horseman galloped around the side of the hunting lodge and rode off after Grendel.

It was Kurster, the Count's giant henchman.

Across his saddle-bow lay the furiously struggling figure of Romana.

10

Count Grendel Plans a Wedding

Zadek ran to the door. 'Get the men mounted, Farrah. After them!'

The Doctor held them back. 'You'll never catch him now. He'll be well on the way to Castle Gracht.' The Doctor shook his head ruefully. 'You know, one almost has to admire the man.'

'Admire him!' spluttered Zadek. 'We should have killed him the minute he walked in here, flag of truce or no flag of truce.'

'He's certainly not short of courage, sir,' said Farrah. 'I mean, riding up like that, distracting us while his man breaks in and kidnaps Lady Romana. It took nerve.'

'Nerve is something Count Grendel has never been short of,' said Zadek grimly.

The Doctor was examining the remains of the shattered android. 'Blown to bits, I'm afraid. Must have been an explosive charge in that spear-head. Trust Grendel to convert a flag of truce into a weapon of war!'

Farrah sighed despondently. 'I can see why he wanted to destroy the android. But why kidnap Lady Romana?'

The Doctor sighed. 'I imagine he's thought up yet another scheme to gain the throne. You've got to admit he's a trier!'

Count Grendel flung open the dungeon door, and thrust Romana inside. 'Romana!' Prince Reynart stirred, and opened his eyes. 'Romana! I thought you'd escaped . . .'

'She did,' snapped Count Grendel viciously. 'But I knew you couldn't live without her, Your Majesty, so I brought her back to you.'

Romana glared angrily at him. 'Do you have to torment him?'

Count Grendel was hurt. 'Now that really is most unfair, my dear. Especially when I've gone to so much trouble to reunite His Majesty with his bride-to-be!'

'His *what*? What are you up to now?'

Count Grendel gave her one of his peculiarly sinister smiles. 'Congratulations! You'll make a lovely couple.'

He went out, slamming the door behind him.

Romana looked down at the Prince. 'What was all that about? What's his idea now?'

'Count Grendel has always had only one idea,' said Reynart feebly. 'He wants to become the rightful, *legal*, King of Tara. If you pose as Princess Strella and marry me, you will automatically become Queen. Five minutes after the wedding, you'll almost certainly become a widow. Whereupon Count Grendel, that well-known protector of widows and orphans will step in and marry you.'

Romana was beginning to understand the plan. 'Thus becoming the Consort of the rightful Queen of Tara. Then I suppose it will be my turn to have an unfortunate accident?'

'Precisely. According to the Laws of Tara, the crown will pass to Grendel. Count Grendel is a great stickler for legality—when it suits him.'

Romana added, 'But Grendel's got the real Princess Strella. Why doesn't he force *her* to marry him?'

Prince Reynart lay back, exhausted. 'I imagine he's tried, and it didn't work. Princess Strella is a very strong-minded girl.'

Count Grendel sat on a throne in the great hall of Castle Gracht. He had ordered the throne to be made some time ago; it would come in handy when Castle Gracht was a Royal Residence. Till poured wine. The Count drank, spat it out, and hurled the silver goblet at Till's head. 'You call this wine? It's vinegar!'

It was at this rather unfortunate moment that the Archimandrite was brought in by two of Count Grendel's guards. The old man looked up at Grendel and said peevishly, 'What is so urgent that I must be dragged from my duties like this? Your men were most insistent.'

Count Grendel rose, and delivered a swift kick to the departing Till. 'Fetch good wine, dog!' He turned to the Archimandrite and said urbanely. 'Forgive me, Your Eminence, but there is a ceremony you must perform.'

'Here? What ceremony.'

'A marriage.'

The Archimandrite shook his head disapprovingly. 'Your own chaplain could have done that for you.'

'Not this marriage.'

'Why? Who is to be married, and to whom?'

'The King of Tara,' said Count Grendel impressively. 'To the Princess Strella.'

'The King is here?'

Count Grendel's voice was grave. 'He has placed himself under my protection, Your Eminence. Sadly, I have to tell you that he is seriously ill—in fact, he is very near to death.'

The old man was shocked. 'I noticed he looked unwell at the Coronation. Not himself at all.'

'Exactly what I thought myself, Archimandrite.'

'But near to death, you say?'

'Indeed he is,' said Count Grendel sadly. 'In fact, it would be as well if you stayed on at Castle Gracht for a while after the ceremony. I fear we shall need you for the funeral rites, soon after the wedding.' Count Grendel brightened. 'Now that I come to think of it, you might as well perform the second wedding straight after the funeral.'

By now the Archimandrite was totally baffled. 'A *second* wedding? And whose, may I ask, will that be?'

'Mine,' said Count Grendel happily. 'I shall be marrying the poor King's widow.'

The Doctor sat brooding in the hunting lodge. With him was K9, who had been forced to make a wide detour to avoid a patrol of Count Grendel's guards. Now K9 had finally arrived, belated but unharmed. At the table, Zadek and Farrah were studying a map of Castle Gracht and its surroundings. 'We can post the men *here*, sir,' Farrah was saying.

Zadek frowned. 'And leave our left flank open to attack? No, *here*, surely.' They seemed to be enjoying themselves so much that the Doctor felt it was a shame to interrupt them. 'How long do you two think it will take to capture the castle, then?'

'Hard to say,' said Zadek gloomily. 'The last siege of Castle Gracht went on for over two years.'

'Well, I haven't got two years to spare,' said the Doctor firmly. 'Besides, Grendel will kill Romana and the Prince long before then.' He leaned over the map. 'I can tell you now, there's only one way to get into that castle quickly.'

'What's that?' demanded Zadek.

'Someone will have to get in and open the gates from the inside. Then your men can charge straight in, take the guard by surprise, and rescue the prisoners before Count Grendel's got time to kill them.'

'That's hardly according to the Rules of War,' objected Farrah.

Zadek snorted. 'Have you ever known Grendel to abide by the Rules of War? It's a good plan, Doctor, but who is going to open the gates?'

'I am.'

'Just you? One man alone?'

The Doctor smiled. 'Well, one man and his dog, anyway. Come on K9!'

Count Grendel strode along the dank stone corridors of his castle, a guard at his heels. He paused outside the door to the first cell. The Prince was sleeping, uneasily. Romana sat beside him, mopping his forehead. 'Very touching,' muttered Grendel. He moved on to the second cell. 'Open!' The guard opened the door and Count Grendel went inside.

Princess Strella was still busy at her endless tapestry. Count Grendel bowed. 'Your Highness.'

Princess Strella ignored him.

Grendel's face darkened, but he managed to keep his voice civil. 'I have come to offer you one last chance to change your mind, Your Highness.'

Princess Strella looked up. 'Never!' She returned to her tapestry.

Count Grendel said persuasively, 'The Archimandrite is here. The King is here. It will all be quite simple.'

Princess Strella was a placid, rather dull girl, but she had generations of Royal training behind her, and an immovable sense of duty. 'I have already told you,

Grendel,' she said precisely. 'I will not marry the King under these circumstances—and I will not marry you under *any* circumstances.'

Count Grendel tried to be jovial. 'Come, come, my dear, surely you want to be Queen?'

The Princess laid down her embroidery. 'As long as I can frustrate your evil schemes by refusing to marry the King, then his life is safe.'

'His life matters so much to you?'

'More than my own,' said the Princess matter-of-factly. 'That is why I will not go through with any marriage under your roof. You may kill me if you wish.'

'I may well do that,' roared Grendel, his mask of urbanity slipping at last. 'I have a substitute, Princess Strella. You have become dispensable!'

He stormed out, and the guard locked the cell.

Princess Strella sighed, and picked up her embroidery. Count Grendel hammered his fist on the door of the neighbouring cell. 'Open it, you fool,' he bellowed. The horrified guard hurried to obey.

Romana looked up from the unconscious Prince. 'You've got to give him proper quarters, Count Grendel. He's getting weaker all the time.'

Grendel nodded sadly. 'Such a pity. I fear he is not long for this world.'

'Nonsense. All he needs is proper quarters, **proper treatment——**'

'I know exactly what he needs, my dear.' Grendel prodded the Prince in the ribs with the toe of his boot.

'As long as he has enough energy left for the marriage ceremony.'

Prince Reynart opened his eyes. 'Never, you hear me. Grendel? Never!'

Count Grendel sighed. 'Come now, Your Majesty, I'm sure you wouldn't wish to be the cause of Princess Strella's death? And no more would you, my dear Romana.'

Romana looked steadily at him. 'All right, Count Grendel. Exactly what do you mean?'

'Princess Strella is in the dungeon next to this one. She is quite well, and quite safe—for the moment.'

'If you harm her, Grendel,' cried the Prince feverishly.

'What? What can you do?' sneered Grendel. His voice hardened. 'Now be quiet, both of you, and listen to me. I had everything arranged, before Romana and her friend the Doctor interfered. Madame Lamia was preparing another android, a perfect copy of the Princess for you to marry.' Count Grendel sighed. 'It would all have been so delightfully simple. You would have married the android with full public ceremony— and she would have killed you on your wedding night. After your unfortunate death, she would have married me.'

Romana was tired of Grendel and his elaborate schemes. 'Well, if you think I'm going to help you by marrying the Prince, you can think again.'

'Oh, but you will,' whispered Grendel, 'I know you will. You will both do exactly as I say—because if you refuse, the real Princess will die!' He paused, savouring their distress, then purred, 'Now what have you to say to that?'

Appalled at the extent of Count Grendel's ruthlessness, Romana and the Prince were too shocked to speak.

Count Grendel resumed his usual polished manner. 'Good, I was sure you'd see reason. I shall send servants to prepare you for the ceremony. Be ready.'

He turned and left the cell.

Prince Reynart slumped back in despair. 'What now, Romana? It doesn't make any difference whether we do what he wants or not—he's going to kill us eventually anyway.'

Romana glanced up at the high barred window. 'Don't give up,' she whispered. 'It's getting dark, and we've still got friends outside. All we can do now is play for time.'

11

Attack by Night

The night was dark and moonless and the massive bulk of Castle Gracht loomed dimly against scudding storm-clouds.

Zadek and Farrah lowered the flat-bottomed punt into the moat of Castle Gracht. It had been brought from the nearby river, at the Doctor's suggestion, carried overland by Zadek's men.

'Right,' said the Doctor. 'In you go, K9!'

Zadek held the boat close to the side of the bank, while Farrah helped the Doctor to lower K9 into it. Once K9 was safely installed in the bottom of the boat, the Doctor jumped in after him, and picked up the paddle from the floorboards.

'The old water-gate is right under the wall opposite,' whispered Zadek. 'Those door timbers are at least a foot thick I'm afraid. They were made to stand up to a battering ram.'

'They won't stand up to K9 though,' said the Doctor confidently. 'Don't worry, we'll manage. You just make sure your chaps are ready to charge, the moment that drawbridge comes down.'

Farrah produced a sword and handed it to the Doctor. 'Here, take this. You may need it!'

'I hope not,' said the Doctor, but he took the sword, tied a knot in his coat-belt, and thrust the sword through it. 'Here we go then.'

Zadek pushed the boat off from the shore. 'We'll be waiting, Doctor. Good luck!'

The Doctor paddled away.

Swiftly and silently, he drove the boat across the smooth, black surface of the moat, taking care to dip the paddle blade in the water without splashing.

There was a nasty moment when a patrolling sentry gazed down at the moat from the battlement, but the boat glided beneath him silent and unseen.

A few minutes later the prow of the punt bumped gently against a heavy arched door, set into the castle wall just above the waterline.

'This must be it, K9,' whispered the Doctor. He grabbed an iron ring set into the massive timbers and steadied the boat.

'Affirmative, Master,' K9's electronic voice was shockingly loud in the night silence.

'Sssh they'll hear us. All right, K9—start cutting!'

K9 moved to the front of the boat, and focused his laser beam on the door.

The massive wooden timbers began to smoke.

In the Great Hall of Gracht, Till and Kurster were making the preparations for the wedding. They were simple enough, a carved wooden table to serve as the

Archimandrite's altar, a few chairs for those of Count Grendel's guards who would act as witnesses. It would be a simple ceremony.

Count Grendel strode into the hall and looked around. 'Is everything ready?'

Till ducked his head. 'Almost my lord.'

'There must be no hitches in the ceremony—in either of the ceremonies!'

Prince Reynart's funeral service was due to follow shortly after his wedding.

'Kurster!' roared Count Grendel.

'Yes, my lord?'

'Make sure the guards are alert. If the Doctor and his friends attack, it may well be tonight. At the first sign of trouble, get down to the dungeons and deal with Princess Strella. You understand me?'

'I do, my lord.' It wouldn't be the first murder Kurster had carried out at Grendel's orders.

'Good. I shall deal with the King and his interfering friend myself.'

Count Grendel looked up as the Archimandrite tottered into the hall. 'Ah, there you are, Your Eminence. Are you ready?'

'I am.' The old man looked round in puzzlement. 'But where are the happy couple?'

'They are in their quarters,' said Count Grendel smoothly. 'I will inform them that you are ready. I shall conduct them here myself.'

Summoning two guards, Count Grendel made his way down to the dungeons, where he found Romana and Prince Reynart submitting unwillingly to the ministrations of his servants. The Prince's wound had been redressed, and he had been given a fresh uniform to wear. Romana was wearing one of Princess Strella's gowns, taken from the baggage captured with the Princess.

Count Grendel surveyed them approvingly. 'Splendid, splendid! But why spoil the effect by looking so miserable, Your Highness? This should be the happiest day of your life. It will probably be the last day too, you might just as well enjoy it!'

He led them into the corridor and paused by the door to the adjoining cell. 'Remember now—no trouble or Strella dies. That I promise. Now, cheer up, it will soon be over.' He took Romana's arm. 'I'm sorry there's no bridal march, my dear, but we're ringing the castle bell.'

The strange wedding party moved away.

The sonorous pealing of a bell came rolling out from the castle tower. 'Hear that, K9?' whispered the Doctor. 'It means either a wedding or a funeral.' He looked at the heavy gate, which was charred and blackened but by no means destroyed. 'Hurry up, can't you? A hamster with a blunt penknife could do it quicker.'

K9 was hurt. 'You ordered no noise, Master.'

'Get on with it K9!'

K9 increased the intensity of his laser beam. The

gate-timbers began to crackle, and some of them burst into flame.

Balancing precariously in the boat, the Doctor kicked at the door. Most of the timbers fell away in blazing sparks. 'About time! Now listen, K9, there's bound to be a lot of stairs, and I've no time to carry you. You'd better stay here, I may need to bring the prisoners out this way if anything goes wrong.'

'Affirmative, Master.'

'And don't fall in the water.'

'I am familiar with boats, Master,' said K9 huffily.

The Doctor patted him on the head. 'You old sea dog, you!' He crawled carefully through the smouldering gap, and looked back at K9. 'Now, don't forget, stay on guard here—and be careful!'

The Doctor disappeared.

'Master?' called K9.

There was a crash from somewhere inside the hole, an indignant cry of 'Sssh, K9,' and then silence.

'Master?' called K9. 'You have forgotten to secure the boat!'

But the Doctor was gone.

Flanked by sword-bearing guards, Romana and Prince Reynart followed Count Grendel into the hall. He led them up the improvised aisle to the table, behind which stood the Archimandrite. In a quavery voice the old man said, 'You will both kneel!'

Romana and Prince Reynart did not move.

Count Grendel glared. 'Remember the Princess,' he hissed. 'Now, kneel!'

They knelt.

The Archimandrite began the ceremony.

The Doctor hurried through the lower corridors of the castle, looking for the dungeon where Romana was confined. He found it at last, but it was empty, the door standing open. He glanced in the next cell, where Princess Strella was still placidly embroidering, and decided to rescue her later. He hurried up the stairs that led to the great hall.

After a good deal of preliminary mumbling from the Archimandrite, the marriage ceremony had now reached the most vital part. 'Do you, Reynart, King of Tara, take this woman, the Princess Strella to be your lawful wedded wife?'

There was a long pause. Reynart caught Count Grendel's menacing look and said weakly, 'I do.'

Romana was wondering desperately what to do for the best. If she went through with the ceremony, then Count Grendel would be able to go on with his evil plans. If she refused, and denounced him, then he would kill them both and probably Strella and the Archimandrite too.

The Archimandrite turned towards her. 'And do you, Strella, Princess of the Royal House of Tara, take this man, Reynart, King of Tara, to be your lawful wedded husband?'

A voice from the back of the hall shouted, 'No, she doesn't!'

Joyfully Romana turned. 'Doctor!'

The Doctor was standing in the doorway smiling at her. 'Hullo, everybody, sorry I'm late. If there's one thing I always enjoy, it's a good wedding, isn't that right, Romana?'

The Archimandrite stared at the kneeling girl before him. 'Romana? What do you mean, Romana? This is the Princess Strella.'

'Oh no, it isn't,' said the Doctor cheerfully. 'Have you got to that bit where you ask if anyone knows any just cause or impediment yet? When you do, I've got news for you!'

Count Grendel strode towards the Doctor, his voice shaking with anger. 'You seem to make a habit of interfering in my affairs, Doctor.'

The Doctor was quite unabashed. 'Yes, I do rather, don't I?'

Suddenly there was a sword in Count Grendel's hand. 'However, *this* will be the last time!'

'Stop,' shouted the horrified Archimandrite. 'Let there be no brawling. This is a solemn ceremony of marriage ...'

'Not any more it isn't,' said Romana. She jumped to her feet, and helped Prince Reynart to stand up.

Guards were converging on the Doctor from all over the great hall, and soon he was ringed by Count Grendel's men. One of them raised a crossbow.

'Doctor, look out!' yelled Romana.

The Doctor prepared to duck, but it was Count Grendel himself who struck the guard's crossbow aside. 'Leave him. He's mine.'

Count Grendel's sword made patterns of light around the Doctor's body. 'Defend yourself, sir!'

'It would be easier if I had a sword,' said the Doctor mildly.

Grendel reached forward and snatched the sword from the Doctor's belt. 'I have no wish to kill a man without a weapon in his hand. I shall give you just one fencing lesson before you die.'

Sword in hand, Count Grendel advanced upon the Doctor.

Prince Reynart gripped Romana's arm. 'Don't look, my dear. Grendel is the finest swordsman on Tara, a Swordmaster of the Ninth Degree. I'm afraid your friend doesn't stand a chance.'

Count Grendel took up the classic fencing stance, left hand on his hip for balance, right hand and right foot extended.

The Doctor stood looking down at the sword in his own hand as if he was wondering how it had got there, and what it was for ...

Grendel's sword flashed forward in a classic lunge— and the Doctor's blade came up and parried it, almost negligently. There was a crackle of energy as the electro-swords clashed together and then sprang apart.

Grendel lunged again. Again the Doctor parried with careless ease.

'He can do it!' gasped Romana. 'He can actually do it.'

Grendel stepped back, angry and baffled. 'My congratulations, Doctor. Already you improve.'

He sprang forward to the attack.

By now Count Grendel was over the shock of surprise and was fighting seriously, with all the formidable skill at his command. The Doctor was now hard put to defend himself.

Count Grendel attacked like a whirlwind, thrusting, slashing, lunging, and the Doctor was driven steadily back.

Romana stood biting her lip, wondering if for once the Doctor had over-reached himself.

But the fury of Count Grendel's assault could not last and he began to tire.

Abruptly, the Doctor started to counter-attack, driving Count Grendel back and back with a series of brilliant lunges and ripostes. The Doctor's sword flicked forward and scored a hit on the Count's chest.

Grendel looked down in astonishment, wondering why he wasn't dead. He realised that the Doctor hadn't even bothered to switch his electro-sword to killing-strength. He was using the lowest setting, the one used for fencing lessons, so that each touch produced no more than a slight tingle.

Enraged by this sign of contempt, Grendel sprang forward with renewed fury. The Doctor's blade slid forward, somehow wrapped itself *around* the other and suddenly the sword was twitched from Count Grendel's hand. It fell clattering to the stone-flagged floor.

Count Grendel drew himself upright, gasping, waiting for the killing thrust.

The Doctor stepped back, and bowed mockingly.

Count Grendel gave him an unbelieving look, then snatched up the sword and returned to the attack.

He fought on doggedly, but now he was fighting in retreat, waiting for the moment to spring aside, and have the Doctor shot down.

From the back of the hall Kurster saw only that the fight was going badly for his master.

He remembered the Count Grendel's instructions— if anything went wrong, Princess Strella was to be killed.

Moving silently for a man of his size, Kurster slipped from the hall on his murderous errand.

12

Victory

Everyone in the great hall was watching the flashing sword-blades as if hypnotised.

Romana knew that the danger wasn't over. If Count Grendel couldn't win by fair means he would certainly try foul—if he could separate himself from the Doctor long enough to shout an order, a dozen cross-bolts would blow the Doctor to pieces.

For the moment, it was only the Doctor's flickering, deadly sword-blade that was keeping Grendel too busy to carry out his treachery. But the moment was bound to come ... Anyone who would threaten to murder an innocent hostage like Princess Strella.

Romana looked round the hall—and saw Kurster slipping away.

She gave an agonised look at the Doctor, then turned and ran out of the hall.

The fight raged on.

Suddenly, the Doctor sprang, jamming his sword hilt against the Count's, pinning him against the wall. 'Where's the gate control?'

Count Grendel glared defiantly at him, and said nothing.

Prince Reynart gathered his strength for one last effort. Grabbing the watching Till by the throat, he shook him vigorously. 'The gate control—where is it?'

Terrified, Till nodded towards a switch set high in a pillar.

'Over there, Doctor,' shouted the Prince. 'On the pillar, just to your right.'

The Doctor thrust Count Grendel away, and sprang for the pillar. Count Grendel sprang after him like a tiger, but he was too late. The Doctor flicked up the row of switches with his left hand—and turned to deflect Grendel's savage lunge with an elegant parry.

Anger gave Count Grendel new strength and he attacked again.

The fight raged on.

Waiting at the head of their troops, Zadek and Farrah saw the drawbridge come smoothly down, the portcullis gate slide up.

'He's done it, sir,' said Farrah exultantly.

Zadek rose to his feet. 'Forward!' he shouted. 'Charge!' Sword in hand he led his men across the bridge.

Princess Strella had put aside her big tapestry frame. There seemed little point in a task she probably wouldn't live to finish. She was embroidering a very small lace handkerchief.

She wasn't particularly surprised when her cell door

was flung open, and Kurster appeared, sword in hand. She waited calmly, as he raised his sword and moved towards her. Something about her calmness unnerved Kurster—and for a second he hesitated.

In that second, Romana appeared in the doorway behind him. She looked round for a weapon, saw the heavy wooden tapestry frame leaning against a bench by the wall, snatched it up and smashed it down hard.

Kurster staggered, and stood swaying ...

Instantly, the Princess seized the water jug from her table and brought it down on Kurster's head with all her strength.

Kurster slid slowly down the wall and on to the bench, upright, but completely unconscious.

Princess Strella looked up, saw Romana's face, and showed real astonishment for the first time in her captivity. 'Who are you?'

Romana smiled. 'I'm afraid that's a very long story.'

When he heard the shouts of Zadek's men in the courtyard, Count Grendel knew everything was over. Deliberately, he began retreating before the Doctor's attack, up the stone staircase, through the narrow door at the top, and out on to the path that ran along the edge of the battlements.

The sound of fighting drifted up from below them. The Doctor stepped back—though he kept his guard well up, just in case. 'Listen to that Grendel. It's all over. That's Zadek and his men. You might just as well surrender.'

'Surrender to that blockhead?' said Grendel scornfully. 'I'm a Gracht, Doctor. We never surrender. We prefer to live to fight another day.'

Count Grendel sprang lightly up on to the battlements, and gazed at the still waters far below. 'Nothing like a midnight swim. I'll finish giving you that fencing lesson, Doctor—one day.'

Hurling his sword at the Doctor's head, Count Grendel dived from the battlements.

Sweeping the flying blade aside with his own, the Doctor went to the edge of the battlements. He was just in time to see Grendel slide smoothly into the water and start swimming towards the woods that bordered the moat.

Possibly some of Zadek's men would capture him— but somehow the Doctor doubted it. He raised his blade in a swordsman's salute, with a kind of reluctant admiration for Count Grendel's consistency. All in all, he'd seldom met a more thoroughgoing villain in all his lives.

Things were very much under control by the time the Doctor got back into the great hall. Count Grendel's men had been disarmed and made prisoner, and Zadek and Farrah were hovering anxiously around the Prince Reynart—King Reynart, he was now, thought the Doctor. Reynart seemed to be recovering strength rapidly now that he was free again.

The Doctor raised his sword in greeting. 'Ah, there you all are! Everyone all right?'

There was a bubble of greetings and congratulations.

'I owe you my life, Doctor,' said the King. 'How can I ever repay you?'

'Oh it was nothing, really. Glad to have been of service.'

Zadek seized the Doctor by the hand. 'Such swordsmanship! His Majesty has told me how valiantly you fought. I never thought I'd live to see anyone beat Grendel of Gracht.'

The Doctor looked surprised. 'Oh really? Was he supposed to be good at it?'

'Doctor, stay here,' said the Prince emotionally. 'This castle and all its lands shall be yours ... Any position in my realm you care to ask for.'

'Well, that's very nice of you, Your Majesty, but I do have a rather pressing appointment on the other side of the galaxy.' He looked round. 'Has anyone seen Romana?'

'She followed Kurster out,' said the King slowly. He leaped to his feet. 'Princess Strella! He went to kill Strella!'

'Where?' asked the Doctor swiftly.

'In the dungeons. Wait for us, Doctor!'

The Doctor was already on his way.

Romana and the Princess were sitting side by side, heads bent over the Princess's embroidery. 'So many different types of stitch,' Romana was saying. 'It must take years to learn.'

'Nonsense, my dear,' said Princess Strella placidly. 'All it takes is patience, and a certain delicacy of touch.

I'm sure you could pick it up in no time. Go on, that's right ...'

Romana completed a stitch, and the Princess nodded. 'Very good!'

The Doctor burst into the dungeon sword in hand and saw Kurster slumped on the bench. He whipped up his sword. 'Don't move!'

Kurster didn't.

The Doctor prodded him in the chest with the tip of the blade. Kurster toppled over sideways and slumped to the ground.

The Doctor threw his sword aside with a sigh of relief. He looked at the girl doing the embroidery. 'You must be Princess Strella.'

The other woman said, 'No, I'm Princess Strella.'

'How do you do?' said the Doctor politely. 'Well, if you're Princess Strella, *this* must be Romana. Sorry to drag you away, Romana, but we've got some rather important business. I suggest you get back into your own clothes and come and help me.'

'The segment,' gasped Romana. She hurried into the next cell, and began changing.

As the Doctor waited in the corridor, the King came hurrying towards the cell, Zadek and Farrah close behind him.

The Doctor moved aside, and the King stepped into the cell, and took the Princess in his arms. 'Strella, you're safe ... and you're real.'

Zadek and Farrah looked discreetly away as the Royal couple kissed.

The Doctor smiled. All in all, he thought, it made a pleasingly romantic conclusion to the entire adventure.

Romana came out of the other cell, now back in the costume in which she'd arrived. 'Come on, Doctor. Let's find that crystal again, and slip away before they make you a Duke or something. Last time I saw it was in that android surgery place.'

A short time later, Romana stood staring around the android surgery in despair. 'It's gone, Doctor. The segment is gone. Grendel must have taken it.'

'Try the Tracer,' suggested the Doctor blandly.

'Of course!' Romana snatched out the Tracer, and waved it around the room. The electronic bleep rose to maximum—and the Tracer was pointing straight at the Doctor.

He grinned and took the crystal from his pocket.

'Oh, very funny, Doctor!'

'And very careless of you. I picked it up on my way in here!'

The Doctor put the crystal back in his pocket. 'Shall we go?'

Romana said, 'It's funny you know, Doctor, but in spite of everything, I'll be sorry to leave Tara.'

'Sorry to leave Tara?' The Doctor was indignant. 'I didn't even catch a fish. Come on!'

As they walked towards the drawbridge, Romana asked, 'Talking of forgetting things, Doctor—what have you done with K9?'

The Doctor gave a gasp of horror. 'K9!' He ran for

the drawbridge and begun running along the path that fringed the side of the castle moat, heading for the rear of the castle. Romana followed him.

As they ran around to the back of the castle they heard a pathetic electronic voice. 'Master! Master! Master!'

K9 was standing in the boat which had drifted right into the centre of the moat. He was marooned, and helpless.

The Doctor found a rope and grappling hook in the castle gatehouse. After several unsuccessful attempts, he managed to hook the edge of the boat and pull K9 to shore.

Watching him, Romana suddenly burst out laughing. 'There you are, Doctor. You managed to catch a fish on Tara after all!'

They drew K9 in, soothed his ruffled feelings, and headed for the TARDIS.

Another part of their dangerous quest was over—but there were still two more segments to be found.

As the Doctor opened the TARDIS door, Romana wondered where the next adventure would lead them.

The Doctor ushered Romana and K9 into the TARDIS, and followed them inside.

With a wheezing groaning sound, the TARDIS dematerialised.

The Doctor and his friends were on their way.